Dear Reader,

Great news—in February 2013 Harlequin Presents Extra is merging with Presents so you will now be able to find more of your favorite authors in one place as Presents increases from six books a month to eight.

There will be more of the themes you love such as secret babies, marriages of convenience, scandalous affairs, all with exciting international settings and delicious alpha heroes. You can also look forward to linked books by some of your most-loved authors and a new exciting eight-book continuity starting in May.

So remember, starting in February there will be eight new Presents books available each month!

Happy reading!

The Presents Editors

P.S. Also available this month:

#3107 A RING TO SECURE HIS HEIR
Lynne Graham

#3108 THE RUTHLESS CALEB WILDE
The Wilde Brothers
Sandra Marton

#3109 BEHOLDEN TO THE THRONE
Empire of the Sands
Carol Marinelli

#3110 THE INCORRIGIBLE PLAYBOY
The Legendary Finn Brothers
Emma Darcy

#3111 BENEATH THE VEIL OF PARADISE
The Bryants: Powerful & Proud
Kate Hewitt

#3112 AT HIS MAJESTY'S REQUEST
The Call of Duty
Maisey Yates

Harry straightened up and, tapping her cheek in passing, his eyes twinkled as he said, "That's my girl!"

She barely stopped her hand from clapping her cheek to rid it of his electric touch. She clenched it into a fist and swiftly decided there would have to be some rules made about this short-term job on the island— like no touching. No kissing on the cheek, either. He was altogether too cavalier about taking liberties with her.

Elizabeth was his stand-in manager, *not his girl!*

She was never going to be *his girl*.

She needed to find herself a serious man to share all that could be shared.

There was no hope of that happening with a playboy like Harry.

In fact, he'd been quite masterful in manipulating people into complying with what he wanted. She would have to watch that particular skill of his and not fall victim to any manipulation that would end up with her in the playboy's bed!

Emma Darcy

THE INCORRIGIBLE PLAYBOY

The Legendary
FINN BROTHERS

HARLEQUIN®

entertain, enrich, inspire™

Recycling programs
for this product may
not exist in your area.

ISBN-13: 978-0-373-23880-4

THE INCORRIGIBLE PLAYBOY

Copyright © 2013 by Emma Darcy

www.Harlequin.com

Printed in U.S.A.

The Legendary
FINN BROTHERS

Australia's most eligible billionaires!

Everyone has heard of **Harry Finn's** reputation:
Utterly ruthless in the pursuit of beautiful women,
his devilishly charming smile is virtually irresistible!
What he wants, he gets—and top of his list is
secretary Elizabeth Flippence....

Notorious for being merciless in the boardroom
tycoon **Michael Finn** is all work and no play.
Distractions aren't on his agenda—especially in the
too-tempting shape of bubbly,
beautiful Lucy Filippence....

Look out for Michael's story—coming soon
from Presents®.

Other titles by Emma Darcy available in ebook:

Harlequin Presents®

Dear Reader,

I want to dedicate this book to Marilyn Callaghan who was my personal assistant, dear friend and traveling companion for eighteen marvellous years together. She was involved in the writing of more than sixty Emma Darcy books, not only as my muse, but also the person I trusted to keep me on track to deliver the best I could do. It was our friendship that made my writing continue to be a joy in my life.

Last year, when she became very ill and I was too worried about her to be creative, she still kept pushing me to write, coming up with ideas, wanting to be involved with another story. To please her, to try to distract us both from what was happening in the real world, I started this book. All too soon she was hospitalised, and I sat by her bed, reading to her the first few chapters as I finished them. It made her happy to feel she was still part of a world we could make together. I'd just started chapter four when she died, leaving me too bereft to go on with it for months afterward.

But I had to finish it. For Marilyn. The last story that she shared with me. I hope I've got it right for her. I hope you enjoy it. She would want you to.

Love always,

Emma Darcy

CHAPTER ONE

THIRTY.

The big three zero.

If ever there was a birthday to inspire the determination to make a change in her life, this was it.

Elizabeth Flippence assessed her reflection in the mirror with a mixture of hope and anxiety. She'd had her long brown hair cut to just below her ears and layered so that it fluffed out around her face in wild waves with bangs across her forehead. It was a much more modern look and softer, more feminine, but she wasn't sure she should have let the hairdresser talk her into the vibrant auburn colour.

It was certainly striking. Which was probably what she needed for Michael Finn to really notice her today—notice her as a woman instead of taking her for granted as his superefficient personal assistant. She desperately wanted their relationship to shift from its consistently platonic level. Two years was long enough to pine for a man who seemed fixated on not mixing business with pleasure.

Which was ridiculous. They were so well suited to each other. Surely Michael knew that in his heart. It couldn't be more obvious. Her frustration over this stand-off situation had been simmering for months, and Elizabeth had decided that today was the day she was going to try smashing down his guard. This makeover should at least capture his attention.

And the hairdresser was right about the auburn tones making her dark brown eyes look brighter. The new hairstyle also seemed to put her rather long nose in better proportion with the rest of her face. It highlighted her slanted cheekbones in a strangely exotic way and even her slightly wide full-lipped mouth looked more right somehow.

Anyway, it was done now and she fiercely hoped it would promote the desired result. When Michael commented on her changed appearance, she would tell him it was her birthday present to herself and maybe…please, please, please…he would suggest celebrating the occasion by taking her out to lunch, or better still, dinner.

She didn't want to be his Girl Friday anymore. She wanted to be his every day and every night girl. If that didn't start happening... Elizabeth took a long deep breath as she faced the unavoidable truth. Thirty really was the deadline for a woman to give serious consideration to finding a life partner if she wanted to have a family of her own. Michael Finn was her choice but if he didn't respond to her differently today, she'd probably be wasting her time to hope for any change from him in the near future. Which meant she would have to move on, try to meet someone else.

She quickly banished the downer thought. It was imperative to be positive today. Smile and the whole world smiled back at you, she told herself. It was one of Lucy's principles and it certainly worked for her sister, who invariably carved a blithe path through life, using her smile to get her out of trouble. A lot was forgiven with Lucy's smile.

Elizabeth practised her own as she left the bathroom. She was just slipping her mobile phone into her handbag, ready to leave for work when it played her signature call tune.

Quickly flipping it open she lifted it to her ear, anticipating the caller would be Lucy, who had spent the weekend with friends at Port Douglas. Her sister's voice instantly bubbled forth.

'Hi, Ellie! Happy birthday! I hope you're wearing the clothes I bought for you.'

'Thanks, Lucy, and yes, I am.'

'Good! Every woman should look bold and beautiful on their thirtieth birthday.'

Elizabeth laughed. The beautiful butterfly blouse, basically in glorious shades of blue and green but with the wings outlined in brown and enclosing a vivid pattern in red and sea-green and yellow and lime, was definitely eye-catching, especially teamed with the sea-green pencil skirt. The outfit was a far cry from her usual style in clothes, but under Lucy's vehement persuasion, she had let herself be seduced by the gorgeous colours.

'I've had my hair cut, too. And dyed auburn.'

'Wow! Can't wait to see that! I'll be back in Cairns later this morning. I'll drop in at your office for a peek. Got to go now.'

The connection clicked off before Elizabeth could say, 'No, don't!'

It was probably silly but she felt uncomfortable about Lucy visiting her at work and had always deterred her from doing it. Because of Michael. As much as she loved her ditzy younger sister, there was no escaping the fact that men seemed irresistibly drawn to her. Her relationships never lasted long. Nothing with Lucy lasted long. There was always another man, another job, another place to go.

For several moments Elizabeth dithered over calling her sister back, not wanting this day to be spoiled by a possible distraction from herself. Yet, didn't she need to test Michael's feelings for her? He should value her worth above Lucy's honeybee attraction. Besides, he might not even see her sister drop in. The door between her office and his was usually closed.

She didn't feel right about putting Lucy off this morning. It was her birthday and her sister was happy and excited about seeing her. They only had each other. Their mother had died of cancer when they were still in their teens, and their father, who had since settled in Mt Isa with another woman, wouldn't even remember her birthday. He never had.

In any event, Michael would have to meet

Lucy sooner or later if the closer involvement Elizabeth was aiming for came to pass. Accepting this inevitability, she picked up her handbag, slid the mobile phone into its compartment and headed off to work.

The month of August was a pleasant one in Far North Queensland, not too hot to walk the five blocks from the apartment she and Lucy shared to The Esplanade, where the head office of Finn's Fisheries was located. Usually she drove her little car, leaving it in the space allocated for her in the underground car park of her boss's building, but she didn't want to be tied to driving it home today. Much better to be free to do anything.

The thought brought another smile to her face as she strolled along. Michael really was the perfect man for her. Finn's Fisheries was a huge franchise with outlets all around Australia. They not only stocked every possible piece of fishing gear—a lot of it imported—but the kind of clothing that went with it: wetsuits, swimming costumes, shorts, T-shirts, hats. The range of merchandise was fantastic and Michael dealt with all of it. She loved how he never missed a beat, always on top of everything. It was how she liked to be herself. Together they made a great team. He often said so himself.

If he would just see they should take the next step, Elizabeth was sure they could team up for life and make it a very happy one, sharing everything. He was thirty-five. It was time for both of them to start building a far more personal partnership. She couldn't believe Michael wanted to remain a bachelor forever.

In the two years she'd known him his relationships with other women had never lasted long, but Elizabeth reasoned it was because he was a workaholic. It would be different with her. She understood him.

Despite all this positive thinking, her heart fluttered nervously as she entered her office. The door to Michael's was open, which meant he was already in, organising the business of the day. It was Monday, the beginning of a new week. The beginning of something new between them, too, Elizabeth fiercely hoped as she took a deep breath to calm herself and walked purposefully to the opened door.

He was seated at his desk, pen in hand, ticking off items on a sheet of paper, his concentration so total he didn't sense her presence. For a few moments Elizabeth simply gazed at him, loving the clean-cut perfection of the man; the thick black hair kept short so it was never untidy, the straight black eyebrows that gave slashing emphasis to the keen intelligence of his silver-grey eyes. The straight nose, firm mouth and squarish jaw all combined to complete the look of the alpha male he was.

As always he wore a top quality white shirt that showed off his flawless olive skin and undoubtedly he would be wearing classy black trousers—his customary work uniform. His black shoes would be shiny and... he was just perfect.

Elizabeth swallowed hard to clear her throat and willed him to give her the kind of attention she craved.

'Good morning, Michael.'

'Good morn—' His gaze lifted, his eyes widening in shock. His mouth was left slightly agape, his voice momentarily choked by the unexpected sight of an Elizabeth who was not the same as usual.

She held her breath. This was the moment when the only-business attitude towards her had to snap. A host of butterflies invaded her stomach. *Smile*, her mind wildly dictated.

Show him the warmth in your heart, the desire heating up your blood.

She smiled and suddenly he grinned, the silver eyes sparkling with very male appreciation.

'Wow!' he breathed, and her skin tingled with pleasure.

'Great hair! Fabulous outfit, too!' he enthused. 'You've done wonders with yourself, Elizabeth. Does this mean there's some new guy in your life?'

The high that had soared from his first words came crashing down. Associating her makeover with another man meant the distance he kept between them was not about to be crossed. Although…maybe he was tempted. Maybe he was just checking if the coast was clear for him to step in.

She rallied, quickly saying, 'No. I've been unattached for a while. I just felt like a change.'

'Super change!' he warmly approved.

That was better. Warmth was good. Elizabeth instantly delivered the planned hint for him to make his move.

'I'm glad you like it. The clothes are a gift from my sister. It's my birthday. She insisted I had to look bold and beautiful today.'

He laughed. 'Well, you certainly do. And we should celebrate your birthday, too. How about lunch at The Mariners Bar? We can make time for it if we get through this inventory this morning.'

Hope soared again. A lunch for two at one of the most expensive restaurants in Cairns, overlooking the marina full of million-dollar yachts...her heart sang with joy. 'That would be lovely. Thank you, Michael.'

'Book us a table. One o'clock should see us clear.' He picked up a sheaf of papers, holding it out to her. 'In the meantime, if you could check this lot...'

'Of course.'

Business as usual, but there was a rainbow at the end of it today. Elizabeth could barely stop her feet from dancing over to his desk to collect the work that had to be done first.

'Bold and beautiful,' Michael repeated, grinning at her as he handed over the papers. 'Your sister must have a lot of pizzazz.'

It killed the song in her heart. He was supposed to be showing more interest in her, not wondering about Lucy. She shouldn't have mentioned her sister. But there was no taking it back, so she had to live with it.

'Yes, she has, but she's terribly ditzy with

it. Nothing seems to stay in her head long enough to put any order into her life.' It was the truth and she wanted Michael to know it. The thought of Lucy being attractive to him in any way was unbearable.

'Not like you,' he said appreciatively.

She shrugged. 'Chalk and cheese. A bit like you and your brother.'

The words tripped off her tongue before Elizabeth could catch them back. The anxiety about Lucy had caused her control to slip. It wasn't appropriate for her to make any comment about her boss's brother. Normally she would keep her mouth firmly shut about him, despite the heartburn Harry Finn invariably gave her with his playboy patter. She hated it when he came into the office. Absolutely hated it.

Michael leaned back in his chair, his mouth tilted in a musing little smile. 'Working behind a desk is definitely not Harry's thing, but I think you might have the wrong impression of him, Elizabeth.'

'I'm sorry.' She grimaced an apology. 'I didn't mean to...to...'

Now she was lost for words!

'It's okay.' Michael waved off her angst. 'I know he seems very casual about everything but his mind is as sharp as a razor blade and he has his thumb on everything to do with his side of the business.'

Charter boats for deep-sea fishing, dive-boats for tourists wanting to explore the Great Barrier Reef, overseeing the resort they'd built on one of the islands—it was playboy stuff compared to what Michael did. Elizabeth's opinion of Harry Finn didn't shift one iota.

'I'll try to see him in that light in the future,' she clipped out.

Michael laughed. Elizabeth's toes curled. He was so charismatically handsome when he laughed. 'I guess he's been ruffling your feathers with his flirting. Don't let it get to you. He's like that with every woman. It's just a bit of fun.'

Oh, sure! Great *fun*! For Harry Finn.

Elizabeth hated it.

However, she managed to paste a smile on her face. 'I'll keep that in mind,' she said. 'Must get to work now. And I'll book our table at The Mariners Bar.'

'Do that.' Another grin. 'We can discuss brothers and sisters over lunch.'

No way, Elizabeth thought as she walked briskly to her own office, firmly closing the

door behind her to ensure that Michael didn't
see Lucy when she dropped in. She didn't
want her sister sparking any interest in his
mind. Nor did she want Harry Finn intrud-
ing on any part of this special lunch date.
This precious time together had to be about
moving closer to each other on a really personal plane. All her hopes for a future with
Michael Finn were pinned on it.

CHAPTER TWO

TEN thirty-seven.

Elizabeth frowned at the clock on her desk. The arrangement with the coffee shop on the ground floor was for coffee and muffins to be delivered at ten-thirty—black expresso and a chocolate muffin for Michael, cappuccino and a strawberry and white chocolate muffin for her. She skipped breakfast to have this treat and her empty stomach was rumbling for it. It was unusual for the delivery to be late. Michael hated unpunctuality and the shop tenants were well aware of his requirements.

A knock on her door had her scuttling out of her chair to open it, facilitating entry as fast as possible. 'You're late,' she said chidingly, before realising the tray of coffee and muffins was being carried by Harry Finn.

Vivid blue eyes twinkled at her. 'Short

delay while they made coffee for me, too,'
he said unapologetically.

'Fine! You can explain that to Michael,'
she bit out, forcing her gritted teeth open to
get the words out.

'Oh, I will, dear Elizabeth. Never would
I leave a blemish on your sterling record of
getting everything right for him,' he rolled
out in the provocative tone that made her
want to hit him. She was not given to vio-
lence but Harry Finn invariably stirred something explosive in her.

'And may I say you look stunning this
morning. Absolutely stunning!' he rattled
on as he stepped into her office, eyeing her
up and down, his gaze pausing where the
butterfly wings on her blouse framed her
breasts, making her nipples stiffen into bul-
lets. She wished they could be fired at him.
His white T-shirt with tropical fish embla-
zoned on it wouldn't look so sexy on him if
there were black holes through it to his all-
too-manly chest.

'The hair is spectacular, not to mention—'

'I'd rather you didn't mention,' she cut him
off, closing the door and waving him towards
Michael's office. 'Your brother is waiting.'

He grinned his devil-may-care grin. 'Won't kill him to wait a bit longer.'

She crossed her arms in exasperated impatience with him as he strolled over to set the tray down on her desk, then hitched himself onto the edge of it, ignoring any reason for haste. The white shorts he wore emphasised his long, tanned, muscular legs. One of them he dangled at her, teasing her need for proper behaviour.

'A moth turning into a butterfly doesn't happen every day,' he happily remarked. 'I want to enjoy the glory of it.'

Elizabeth rolled her eyes. She was not going to stand for this. A moth! She had never been a moth! She had simply chosen to be on the conservative side with her appearance to exemplify a serious career person, not someone who could ever be considered flighty like her sister.

'The coffee will be getting cold,' she stated in her chilliest voice.

'Love the sea-green skirt,' he raved on. 'Matches the colour of the water near the reef. Fits you very neatly, too. Like a second skin. In fact, it's inspiring a fantasy of you as a mermaid.' He grinned. Evilly. 'I bet you'd swish your tail at me.'

'Only in dismissal,' she shot at him, pushing her feet to walk to the desk and deal with the coffee herself since Harry was not inclined to oblige. It meant she had to go close to him, which she usually avoided because the man was so overwhelmingly male, inyour-face male, that her female hormones seemed to get in a tizzy around him. It was extremely irritating.

He wasn't as classically handsome as Michael. He was more raffishly handsome—his longish black curly hair flopping around his face, crow's-feet at the corners of his eyes from being out in the weather, a slightly crooked nose from having it broken at some point in his probably misspent youth, and a mouth that was all-too-frequently quirked with amusement. At her. As it was now.

'Have you ever wondered why you're so uptight with me, Elizabeth?' he tossed out.

'No. I don't give you that much space in my mind,' she answered, deliberately ignoring him as she removed her coffee and muffin from the tray.

'Ouch!' he said as though she'd hurt him, then laughed to show she hadn't. 'If I ever get too big for my boots, I know where to come to be whipped back into shape.'

She gave him a quelling look. 'You've come to see Michael. Just follow me into his office.'

The devil danced in his eyes. 'Only if you swish your tail at me.'

She glared back. 'Stop playing with me. I'm not going there with you. Not ever,' she added emphatically.

He was totally unabashed. 'All work, no play—got to say you're safe with Mickey on that score.'

Safe? The word niggled at Elizabeth's mind as she carried the tray to Michael's door. Why was Harry so sure she was safe with his brother? She didn't want to be safe. She wanted to be desired so much, there would be no distance left between them.

Harry bounded past her, opened the door and commanded his brother's attention. 'Hi, Mickey! I held up the coffee train to have one made for myself. Have a few things to discuss with you. Here's Elizabeth with it now.'

'No problem,' Michael answered, smiling at her as she sailed in with the tray.

She hugged the smile to her heart. Michael was the man of true gold. Harry was all glitter. And she hated him calling his brother Mickey. It was rotten, schoolboy stuff—

Mickey Finn——linking him to a spiked drink, and totally inappropriate for the position he now held. No dignity in it at all. No respect.

'Thanks, Elizabeth,' Michael said warmly as she unloaded the tray, setting out the two coffees and muffin on his desk. 'Table booked?'

'Yes.'

'What table?' Harry asked, instantly putting her on edge again.

'It's Elizabeth's birthday. I'm taking her out to lunch.'

'A…ha!'

Her spine crawled at the wealth of significance she heard in Harry's voice. If he was about to make fun of the situation… She picked up the emptied tray and swung around to shoot him a killing look.

He lifted his hand in a salute, pretending to plead for a truce between them but his eyes glittered with mocking amusement. 'Happy birthday, dear Elizabeth.'

'Thank you,' she grated out, and swiftly left the two men together for their discussions, closing the door to give them absolute privacy and herself protection from *that man*.

It was difficult to concentrate on work. She tried, but the clock kept ticking on——eleven o'clock, eleven-thirty, twelve. Lucy hadn't dropped in and Harry was still with Michael. Anything could have happened with Lucy. It frequently did. She might not make it into the office at all, which would be a relief, no chance of a meeting with Michael. Harry was the main problem. She wouldn't put it past him to invite himself to her birthday lunch. If he did, would Michael put him off?

He had to.

No way could a romantic mood develop between them if Harry was present. He would spoil everything.

A knock on her door cut off her inner angst. Elizabeth looked up to see the door opening and Lucy's head poking around it.

'Okay to come in?'

Her stomach cramped with nervous tension at the late visit but it was impossible to say anything but 'Yes.'

Lucy bounced in, exuding effervescence as she always did. Today she was dressed in a white broderie anglaise outfit: a little frilly skirt that barely reached midthigh, an off-the-shoulder peasant blouse, a wide tan belt slung around her hips, lots of wooden beads dangling from her neck, wooden bangles travelling up one forearm and tan sandals that were strapped up to mid-calf. Her long blond hair was piled up on top of her head with loose strands escaping everywhere. She looked like a trendy model who could put anything together and look good.

'Ooh...I *love* the hair, Ellie,' she cooed, hitching herself onto the edge of Elizabeth's desk, just as Harry had, which instantly provoked the thought they would make a good pair.

'It's very sexy,' Lucy raved on. 'Gives you that just-out-of-bed tumbled look and the colour really, really suits you. It complements the clothes I picked out for you brilliantly. I have to say you look absolutely marvellous.' Her lovely sherry-brown eyes twinkled with delight. 'Now tell me you *feel* marvellous, too.'

Lucy's smile was so infectious, she had to smile back. 'I'm glad I made the change. How was your weekend?'

'Oh, so-so.' She waved her hand airily then pulled a woeful grimace. 'But I've had the most terrible morning.'

Out of the corner of her eye Elizabeth caught the opening of the door to Michael's office. Tension whipped along her nerves. Was it Harry coming out or both men?

Lucy rattled out her list of woes, her hands making a host of dramatic gestures. 'A body was buried in the wrong plot and I had to deal with that. Then a call came in that someone was interfering with a grave. I had to go out to the cemetery and investigate, but that wasn't too bad. It was only a bereaved husband digging a hole on top of the grave to put in potting soil so he could plant his wife's favourite rose. Nice, really. The worst thing was a dog running amok in the memorial garden and knocking off some of the angels' heads. I had to collect them, load them into the van, and now I have to find someone who can stick them back on again. You wouldn't believe how heavy those angels' heads are.'

'Angels' heads…' It was Michael's voice, sounding totally stunned.

It jerked Lucy's attention to him. 'Oh, wow!' she said, looking Michael up and down, totally uninhibited about showing how impressed she was with him.

Elizabeth closed her eyes and sucked in a deep breath.

'Are you Ellie's boss?' The question popped out with barely a pause.

Elizabeth opened her eyes again to see Michael shaking his head as though bringing himself out of a daze, and Harry behind his shoulder, looking straight at her with a sharp intensity in his bedroom blue eyes she had never seen before. It gave her the weird feeling he was tunnelling into her mind. She quickly dropped her gaze.

'Yes. Yes, I am,' Michael finally answered. 'And you are?'

'Lucy Flippence. Ellie's sister. I work in cemetery administration so I often have to deal with angels.'

'I see,' he said, looking at Lucy as though she was a heavenly apparition.

She hopped off her perch on the desk and crossed the floor to him with her hand extended. 'Pleased to meet you. Okay if I call you Michael?'

'Delighted,' he said, taking her hand and holding on to it as he slowly turned to make the last introduction. 'This is my brother, Harry.'

Elizabeth fiercely willed Lucy to find Harry more attractive. No such luck! Her hand was left in Michael's snug grasp. She raised her other in blithe greeting. 'Hi, Harry!' It was tossed at him in a kind of bubbly dismissal, which meant in Lucy's mind he didn't really count.

'Charmed,' Harry purred at her.

It floated right over her head, no impact at all.

Elizabeth's heart sank like a stone.

Lucy was intent on engaging Michael and he was obviously enthralled with her.

'I don't know if you know but it's Ellie's birthday today and I thought I'd treat her to a really nice lunch somewhere. You won't mind if I take her off and she's a bit late back, will you, Michael?' she said appealingly.

There was a terrible inevitability about what happened next.

'Actually, I'd decided to do the same myself. Lunch at The Mariners Bar.'

'Oh, wow! The Mariners Bar! What a lovely boss you are to take Ellie there!'

'Why don't you join us? It will be a better celebration of her birthday if you do.'

'I'll come, as well. Make a party of it,' Harry put in, instantly supporting the idea.

'I only booked a table for two,' Elizabeth couldn't help saying, even though knowing it was a futile attempt to change what wouldn't be changed now. Her secret dream was already down the drain.

'No problem. I'm sure the maître d' will make room for us,' Michael said, oozing confidence as he smiled at Lucy. 'We'd be delighted to have the pleasure of your company.'

'Well, a foursome should be more fun, don't you think, Ellie?'

The appealing glance over her shoulder forced Elizabeth to smile and say, 'Certainly no awkward silences with you, Lucy.'

She laughed. 'That's settled, then. Thank you for asking me, Michael. And it's good of you to join in the party, too, Harry.'

The death knell to a happy birthday, Elizabeth thought. Not only would she have to watch Michael being fascinated by her sister, she'd also have to put up with Harry getting under her skin all the time. She slid him a vexed look. His mouth quirked at her, seemingly with more irony than amusement, but that probably didn't mean anything. No doubt he was anticipating having heaps of *fun* at her expense.

This lunch was going to be the lunch from hell.

Elizabeth didn't know how she was going to get through it without throwing in the towel, having hysterics and drowning herself in the marina.

CHAPTER THREE

ELIZABETH knew she'd be paired with Harry
for the stroll along the boardwalk to the marina, and she was. There was no point in
trying to fight for Michael's company. His
preference for Lucy to be at his side had
been made so clear, pride dictated that the
arrangement be accepted with as much dignified grace as she could muster.

The two of them walked ahead and it was
sickening watching the connection between
them flourishing. Lucy, of course, was never
short of a word, and Michael was lapping up
every one of them, enjoying her bubbly personality. It wouldn't last, Elizabeth told herself, but that was no consolation. The damage
was done. Lucy had achieved in one minute
flat what she had been unable to draw from
Michael in two years. Even if he turned to

her later on, she would never be able to forget that.

The boardwalk ran along the water's edge of the park adjoining The Esplanade, and she tried to distract herself with the people they passed; couples lounging under the shade of trees, children making use of the play areas set up for them, boys scaling the rock-climb. It was a relief that Harry was leaving her to her silence for a while. It was difficult to cope with him at the best of times, and this was the worst.

She could have chosen to tell Lucy about her secret passion for her boss. That would have warned her off although she wouldn't have understood it. It simply wasn't in Lucy to pine for a man who didn't respond to her as she wanted him to respond. She probably would have looked aghast and said, 'Throw him away, Ellie. He's not that into you if you've waited this long for him to make a move.'

That truth was staring her in the face right now.

And it hurt.

It hurt so badly, she had to keep blinking back the tears that threatened to well into her eyes. Her chest was so tight she could hardly breathe. She'd been a fool to hope, a fool to think today might be the day. It was never going to happen for her.

'Ellie…'

It was a jolt to her wounded heart, hearing Harry speak her childhood name in a low, caressing tone.

'I like it,' he went on. 'Much better than Elizabeth. It conjures up a more carefree person, softer, more accessible.'

Her spine stiffened. He was doing it again, digging at her. She shot him a hard, mocking look. 'Don't get carried away by it. Lucy simply couldn't say Elizabeth when she was little. She calls me Ellie out of habit.'

'And affection, I think.' There was a look of kindness in his eyes that screwed up her stomach as he added, 'She doesn't know she's hurting you, does she?'

Her mind jammed in disbelief over Harry's insightful comment. 'What do you mean?'

He grimaced at her prevarication. 'Give it up, Ellie. You're not Mickey's type. I could have told you so but you wouldn't have believed me.'

Humiliation burned through her. Her cheeks flamed with it. She tore her gaze from the certain knowledge in Harry Finn's and stared at his brother's back—the back Michael had turned on her to be with her sister. How had Harry known what she'd yearned for? Had Michael known, too? She couldn't bear this. She would have to resign from her job, find another.

'Don't worry,' Harry said soothingly. 'You can keep on working for him if you want to. Mickey doesn't have a clue. He's always had tunnel vision—sets his mind on something and nothing else exists.'

Relief reduced some of the heat. Nevertheless, it was still intensely disturbing that Harry was somehow reading her mind. Or was he guessing, picking up clues from her reactions? She hadn't admitted anything. He couldn't really *know*, could he?

'On the other hand, it would be much better if you did resign,' he went on. 'It's never good to keep being reminded of failure. And no need to go job-hunting. You can come and work for me.'

Work for him? Never in a million years! It spurred her into tackling him head-on, her eyes blazing with the fire of battle. 'Let me tell you, Harry Finn, I have never failed at any work Michael has given me and working for you has no appeal whatsoever.'

He grinned at her. 'Think of the pleasure of saying what you think of me at every turn instead of having to keep yourself bottled up around Mickey.'

'I am not bottled up,' she declared vehemently.

He sighed. 'Why not be honest instead of playing the pretend-game? Your fantasy of having Mickey fall at your feet is never going to come true. Face it. Give it up. Look at me as the best tonic for lovesickness you could have. Balls of fire come out of you the moment I'm around.'

'That's because you're so annoying!'

Her voice had risen to a passionate outburst, loud enough to attract Michael's and Lucy's attention, breaking their absorption in each other. They paused in their walk, turning around with eyebrows raised.

'It's okay,' Elizabeth quickly assured them. 'Harry was just being Harry.'

'Be nice to Elizabeth, Harry,' Michael chided. 'It's her birthday.'

'I *am* being nice,' he protested.

'Try harder,' Michael advised, dismissing the distraction to continue his tête-à-tête with Lucy.

'Right!' Harry muttered. 'We need some

control here, Ellie, if you want to pretend there's nothing wrong in your world.'

'The only thing wrong in my world is you,' she muttered back fiercely. 'And don't call me Ellie.'

'Elizabeth reigns,' he said in mock resignation.

She bit her lips, determined not to rise to any more of his baits.

They walked on for a while before he started again.

'This won't do,' he said decisively. 'We'll be at the restaurant soon. If you sit there in glum silence, I'll get the blame for it and that's not fair. It's not my fault that Mickey's attracted to your sister. Your best move is to start flirting with me. Who knows? He might suddenly get jealous.'

This suggestion stirred a flicker of hope. Maybe...

The shared laughter from the couple in front of them dashed the hope before it could take wing. Nevertheless, Harry did have a valid point. If she didn't pretend to be having a good time, even Michael and Lucy would realise this birthday treat was no treat at all for her. She had to *look* happy even though she couldn't *be* happy.

She sighed and slid him a weighing look. 'You know it won't mean anything if I flirt with you.'

'Not a thing!' he readily agreed.

'It's just for the sake of making a cheerful party.'

'Of course.'

'It's obvious that you're a dyed-in-the-wool playboy, and normally I wouldn't have anything to do with you, Harry, but since I'm stuck with you on this occasion, I'll play along for once.'

'Good thinking! Though I take exception to the playboy tag. I do know how to play, which I consider an important part of living—something I suspect you do too little of—but that's not all I am.'

'Whatever...' She shrugged off any argument about his personality. Arguing would only get her all heated again and she needed to be calm, in control of herself. Harry was right about that.

They'd walked past the yacht club and were on the path to the cocktail bar adjoining the restaurant when Harry made his next move.

'Hey, Mickey!' he called out. 'I'll buy the

girls cocktails while you see the maître d'
about our table.'

'Okay' was tossed back at him, his attention reverting to Lucy with barely a pause.

'No doubt about it, he's besotted,' Harry
dryly commented. 'How old are you today,
Elizabeth?'

'Thirty,' she answered on a defeated sigh.
No point in hiding it.

'Ah! The big three zero. Time to make a
change.'

Precisely what she had thought. And still
had to think now that Michael had proved
his disinterest in her personally.

'Go with me on this,' Harry urged.

'Go with you on what?'

'Something I was discussing with Mickey
this morning. I'll bring it up again after
lunch. Just don't dismiss it out of hand. It
would be the perfect change for you.'

'You couldn't possibly know what's perfect for me, Harry,' she said sceptically.

He cocked a teasing eyebrow. 'I might just
be a better judge on that than you think I am.'

She shook her head, her eyes mocking this
particular belief in himself.

He grinned. 'Wait and see.'

She wasn't about to push him on it. Harry

enjoyed being tantalising. Elizabeth had found her best course was simply to show complete disinterest. In this case, she couldn't care less what he had in mind. All she cared about was getting through lunch without showing how miserable she was.

Michael left them at the cocktail bar, striding swiftly into the restaurant to speak to the maître d', obviously in a hurry to get back to Lucy. Harry led them to a set of two-seater lounges with a low table in between and saw them settled with her and Lucy facing each other.

'Now, let me select cocktails for you both,' he said, the vivid blue eyes twinkling confidence in his choices. 'A Margarita for you, Elizabeth.'

It surprised her that he'd actually picked her favourite. 'Why that one?' she asked, curious about his correct guessing.

He grinned. 'Because you're the salt of the earth and I revere you for it.'

She rolled her eyes. The day Harry Finn showed any reverence for her was yet to dawn. He was just making a link to the salt-encrusted rim of the glass that was always used for a Margarita cocktail.

'You're right on both counts,' Lucy happily volunteered. 'Ellie loves Margaritas and she *is* the salt of the earth. I don't know what I'd do without her. She's always been my anchor.'

'An anchor,' Harry repeated musingly. 'I think that's what's been missing from my life.'

'An anchor would only weigh you down, Harry,' Elizabeth put in dryly. 'It would feel like an albatross around your neck.'

'Some chains I wouldn't mind wearing.'

'Try gold.'

He laughed.

'Do you two always spar like this?' Lucy asked, eyeing them speculatively.

'Sparks invariably fly,' Harry claimed.

It was on the tip of her tongue to say she invariably hosed them down, remembering just in time that flirting was the order of this afternoon, so she gave him an arch look and said, 'I would have to admit that being with Harry is somewhat invigorating.'

Lucy laughed and clapped her hands. 'Oh, I love it! What a great lunch we'll all have together!' Her eyes sparkled at Harry. 'What cocktail will you choose for me?'

'For the sunshine girl… A Piña Colada.'

She clapped her hands again. 'Well done, Harry. That's *my* favourite.'

'At your service.' He twirled his hand in a salute to them both and headed off to the bar.

Lucy was beside herself with delight. 'He's just what you need, Ellie. Loads of fun. You've been carrying responsibility for so long, it's well past time you let loose and had a wild flutter for once. Be a butterfly instead of a worker bee.'

At least she didn't say *moth*, Elizabeth thought wryly.

'I might just do that,' she drawled, encouraging the idea there was a connection between her and Harry.

'Go for it,' Lucy urged, bouncing forward on her seat in excitement. 'I'm going for Michael. He's an absolute dreamboat. I'm so glad I wasn't held up any longer at the cemetery. I might have missed out on meeting him. Why didn't you tell me your boss was gorgeous?'

'I've always thought him a bit cold,' she said carefully.

Lucy threw up her hands in exasperation at her sister's lack of discernment. 'Believe me. The guy is hot! He makes me sizzle.'

Elizabeth shrugged. 'I guess it's a matter

of chemistry. Harry is the hot one for me.'
It wasn't entirely a lie. He frequently raised
her temperature...with anger or annoyance.

Lucy heaved a happy sigh. 'Brothers and
sisters...wouldn't it be great if we ended up
together...all happy families.'

Elizabeth's mind reeled from even consid-
ering such a prospect. 'I think that's a huge
leap into the future. Let's just take one day
at a time.'

'Oh, you're always so sensible, Ellie.'

'Which is something I value very highly
in your sister,' Michael declared, picking
up on Lucy's words and smiling warmly at
Elizabeth as he returned, but he seated himself beside Lucy, who instantly switched on
a brilliant smile for him, fulsomely agree-
ing, 'Oh, I do, too. But I also want Ellie to
have fun.'

'Which is where I come in,' Harry said,
also catching Lucy's words as he came back.
His eyes danced wicked mischief at Elizabeth. 'Starting with cocktails. The bartender
will bring them over. Here are the peanuts
and pretzels.'

He placed a bowl of them on the table
and settled himself beside Elizabeth, too
closely for her comfort. She wanted to shift

away and somehow Harry knew it, instantly throwing her a challenging look that made her sit still and suffer his male animal impact. If she was really attracted to him, she would welcome it. Playing this pretend-game was not going to be easy, but she had to now in front of Lucy.

Her sister turned her smile to Harry. 'What cocktail did you order for Michael?'

'A Manhattan. Mickey is highly civilised. He actually forgets about sunshine until it sparkles over him.'

Lucy laughed. 'And yourself?'

'Ah, the open sea is my business. I'm a salty man so I share Elizabeth's taste for Margaritas.'

'The open sea?' Lucy queried.

'Harry looks after the tourist side of Finn's Fisheries,' Michael answered. 'I take care of buying in the stock for all our franchises.'

'Ah!' Lucy nodded, understanding why Harry was dressed the way he was and how very different the brothers were.

Why she was attracted to Michael and not Harry was beyond Elizabeth's understanding. Sunshine and sea should go together. They both had frivolous natures. It wasn't fair that sexual chemistry had struck in the wrong place. Why couldn't it strike sensibly?

The bartender arrived with their cocktails.

Harry handed her the Margarita and clicked his glass against hers. 'Happy Birthday, Elizabeth,' he said warmly, making her squirm inside even as she forced a smile and thanked him.

The others followed suit with their glasses and well-wishing.

Elizabeth settled back against the cushions and sipped her cocktail, silently brooding over the totally non-sensible ironies of life. Was there any reward for being *sensible*? The old saying that *good things come to those who wait* was not proving true for her.

She wondered how long was the life of a butterfly.

Probably very short.

But it might be sweet if she could bring herself to be a butterfly—just cut loose from all her safety nets and fly wild for a while, thinking of nothing but having a good time. She should take a vacation, get right away from whatever was developing between Michael and Lucy, try drowning her misery with mindless pleasures.

The Margarita was good. And it packed

quite a punch. Maybe if she stopped being sensible and had two or three of them, her mind would get fuzzy enough to put this whole situation at an emotional distance, let her float through lunch…like a butterfly.

CHAPTER FOUR

ELIZABETH stared blankly at the luncheon menu. Food. She had to choose something. Her head was swimming from two Margaritas in quick succession. Bad idea, thinking alcohol could fix anything. It didn't help at all.

'I bet I know what you're going to order, Ellie,' Lucy said with a confident grin.

'What?' Any suggestion was welcome.

'The chilli mud crab.'

Chilli. Not today. Her stomach was in too fragile a state.

'Actually, I can't see that on the menu,' Michael said, glancing quizzically at Lucy.

'Oh, I didn't really look. I just assumed,' she quickly defended. No way would she admit that her dyslexia made reading menus difficult. 'What have you decided on, Michael?'

Lucy would undoubtedly choose the same. She was so adept at hiding her disability, hardly anyone ever guessed she had a problem.

'How about sharing a seafood platter for two with me, Elizabeth?' Harry said, leaning closer to point out the platter's contents on the menu. 'You get crab on it, as well as all the other goodies and we can nibble away on everything as we please.'

'Harry will eat the lion's share,' Michael warned.

Yes, Elizabeth thought, relieved to have such ready help, making it easier for her lack of appetite to go unnoticed.

Harry instantly raised a hand for solemn vowing. 'I swear I'll give you first choice of each titbit.'

'Okay, that's a done deal,' she said, closing the menu and slanting her food-rescuer a grateful smile.

'Sealed with a kiss,' he said, bright blue eyes twinkling wickedly as he leaned closer still and pecked her on the cheek.

Her teeth grated together as heat bloomed from the intimate skin contact. The *flirting* agreement flew right out of her mind. His ability to discomfort her on any spot whatsoever had her snapping, 'You can keep that mouth of yours for eating, Harry.'

He gave her his evil grin as he retorted, 'Elizabeth, I live for the day when I'll eat you all up.'

'That'll be doomsday,' she slung back.

'With the gates of heaven opening for me,' Harry retaliated, his grin widening.

Lucy's laughter reminded her just in time that flirting shouldn't have too sharp an edge, so she swallowed her *hell* comment, heaved a long-suffering sigh and shook her head at Harry. 'You are incorrigible.'

'A man has to do what a man has to do,' he archly declared, sending Lucy off into more peals of laughter.

Elizabeth declined asking what he meant.

Nevertheless, as the birthday luncheon progressed, she schooled herself to respond lightly to Harry's banter, pretending to be amused by it, making a show of enjoying his company. At least he was very persistent in claiming her attention, forcefully distracting her from Lucy's and Michael's stomach-curdling absorption in each other, and he did eat the lion's share of the seafood platter without trying to push her into trying more than she could manage.

It was weird finding herself grateful to have Harry at her side, but just this once she actually did. Without him she would feel wretchedly alone, facing the worst scenario of lost hopes. How she was going to cope, hiding her feelings from both Lucy and Michael in the days to come, she didn't know. She hoped they would go off somewhere together after this luncheon, give her some space, release her from the tension of keeping up a happy pretence that everything was fine.

A waiter cleared the table and offered them the sweets menu. Elizabeth decided on the selection of sorbets since they should just slide down her throat without any effort. As soon as the orders were given, Harry leaned an elbow on the table and pointed a finger at his brother, claiming his attention.

'Mickey, I have the solution to my problem with the resort.'

'You have to clear that guy out, Harry,' came the quick advice. 'Once you confront him you can't leave him there. The potential for damage…'

'I know, I know. But it's best to confront him with his replacement. We walk in and turf him out. No argument. A done deal.'

'Agreed, but you don't have a ready replacement yet and the longer he stays…'

'Elizabeth. She's the perfect person for the management job—completely trustworthy, meticulous at checking everything, capable of handling everything you've thrown at her, Mickey.'

Confusion over this brother-to-brother business conversation instantly cleared. *This* was what Harry had intended to bring up after lunch—the perfect change for her. Except it wasn't perfect. Working for him would drive her bats.

'Elizabeth is my PA,' Michael protested.

'I'm in more need of her than you are right now. Lend her to me for a month. That will give me time to interview other people.'

'A month…' Michael frowned over the inconvenience to himself.

A month…

That was a tempting time frame—manageable if Harry wasn't around her all the time. The resort wasn't his only area of interest and responsibility. A month away from Michael and Lucy was a very attractive proposition.

'On the other hand, once Elizabeth gets

her teeth into the job, she might want to stay on,' Harry said provocatively.

No way—not with him getting under her skin at any given moment!

Michael glowered at him. 'You're not stealing my PA.'

'Her choice, Mickey.' Harry turned to her. 'What do you say, Elizabeth? Will you help me out for a month…stay on the island and get the resort running as it should be run? My about-to-be ex-manager has been cooking the books, skimming off a lot of stuff to line his own pockets. You'll need to do a complete inventory and change the suppliers who've been doing private deals with him. It would be a whole new challenge for you, one that…'

'Now hold on a moment,' Michael growled. 'It's up to me to ask Elizabeth if she'll do it, not you, Harry.'

'Okay. Ask her.'

Yes was screaming through her mind. It offered an immediate escape from the situation with Michael and Lucy; no need to explain why she wanted to go away; a whole month of freedom from having to see or talk to either of them; a job that demanded her complete attention, keeping miserable thoughts at bay. These critical benefits made the irritation of having to deal with Harry relatively insignificant. Her heart was not engaged with him. Her head could sort out his effect on her, one way or another.

Michael heaved an exasperated sigh, realising he'd been pushed into a corner by his brother. 'It's true. You would be helping us out if you'd agree to step in and do what needs to be done at the resort,' he conceded, giving Elizabeth an earnest look. 'I have every confidence in your ability to handle the situation. Every confidence in your integrity, too. I hate losing you for a month…'

You've just lost me forever, Elizabeth thought.

'…but I guess someone from the clerical staff can fill in for a while….'

'Andrew. Andrew Cook,' she suggested.

He frowned. 'Too stodgy. No initiative.'

'Absolutely reliable in doing whatever task he's set,' she argued, rather bitchily, liking the fact that Michael found him stodgy. He'd obviously found her stodgy, too, in the female stakes.

'I take it that's a yes to coming to the island with me,' Harry slid in, grinning from ear to ear.

She shot him a quelling look. 'I'm up for the challenge of fixing the management problems, nothing else, Harry.'

'Brilliant!'

He purred the word, making her skin prickle. It instantly gave her the unsettling feeling she might have bitten off more than she could chew with Harry Finn. But he wouldn't be at her side all the time on the island. Going was still better than staying at home.

'That's it, then,' Michael said with a resigned air.

'A whole month! I'll miss you, Ellie,' Lucy said wistfully.

'The time will pass quickly enough,' Elizabeth assured her—*particularly with Michael dancing attendance.*

The waiter arrived with the sweets they'd ordered.

'We need to get moving on this,' Harry muttered as he dug into his chocolate mud cake.

'As soon as possible,' Michael agreed.

'Today,' Harry decided, checking his Rolex watch. 'It's only three o'clock now. We could be over on the island by four-thirty. Have him helicoptered out by six. We leave here when we've finished our sweets, hop on the boat...'

'It is Elizabeth's birthday, Harry,' Michael reminded him. 'She might have other plans for today.'

'No, I'm good to go,' she said, recklessly seizing the chance to be relieved of staying in Michael's and Lucy's company any longer.

'What about clothes and toiletries and stuff?' Lucy put in. 'You're going for a month, Ellie.'

'You can pack for her, Lucy,' Harry said decisively. 'Mickey can take you home, wait while you do it, take Elizabeth's bags and arrange their shipping to the island.'

'No problem,' Michael said, smiling at Lucy like a wolf invited into her home to gobble her up.

Lucy happily agreed with the plan, her eyes sizzling with sexual promises as she smiled back at her new lover-to-be.

Elizabeth shovelled the sorbet down her throat. The faster she got out of here, the better.

'Ready?' Harry asked the moment she put her spoon down.

'Ready,' she answered emphatically, grabbing her handbag and rising to her feet, wanting to run but knowing she had to discipline herself to suffer goodbyes.

Lucy wrapped her in a big hug, mischievously saying, 'Have a lovely time with Harry, Ellie.'

'I will,' she replied through gritted teeth. Denials of that idea would not only be a total waste of time, but also prolong this whole wretched togetherness.

Michael kissed her cheek, wryly murmuring, 'I'll miss you.'

I won't miss you, Elizabeth thought fiercely, barely managing to force a smile. 'Thank you for my birthday lunch, Michael.'

'Pleasure,' he replied, his gaze sliding to Lucy.

'We're off,' Harry said, seizing Elizabeth's hand and pulling her with him.

His hand was strong and hot, wrapping firmly around her fingers, shooting warmth up her arm, but she didn't care if heat travelled to her brain and fried it right now. He was acting fast, taking her to the freedom she needed, and she was grateful for that. Once they were outside, he led her straight to the long wharf where rows of million-dollar yachts were docked on either side.

'Where's your boat?' she asked.

'Right at the end. No shuffling around. A quick, easy getaway. Full throttle to the island.'

'Good!'

He slid her one of his devilish grins. 'I must say I admire your decisiveness.'

She gave him a baleful look. 'Save your chatting up for some other woman, Harry. I played your game in front of Michael and Lucy because it suited me to do it, and I accepted your job offer because that suited me, too. As far as I'm concerned, there's work to be done and I'll do it. I don't expect to have *a lovely time* with you.'

His eyes held hers with a blast of discomforting intensity. 'No, not right now,' he drawled. 'Having had your expectations comprehensively dashed, I daresay you'll be a sourpuss for some time to come. But the island is a lovely place and I hope it will work some magic on you.'

A sourpuss...

The shock of that description halted her feet. She stared back at the blazing blue eyes, hating the knowledge she saw in them, knowledge of her hopes and the humiliation of seeing Michael respond to her sister as he had never—would never—respond to her.

She couldn't wipe away Harry's perception of the situation, couldn't deny the truth, but was that any reason to be sour on him? He'd been her saviour today.

'I'm sorry,' she blurted out. 'I haven't thanked you.'

His sexy mouth moved into an ironic tilt. 'No thanks necessary, Elizabeth.'

His voice was soft, deep, and somehow it made her heart turn over.

She shook her head. 'That's not true, Harry. You were very effective in covering up my…my difficulties with how things went down today. I am grateful to you for rescuing me every time I hit a brick wall.'

'You'll bounce back, Elizabeth. Look on tomorrow as the first day of a new life—a butterfly breaking free of its confining cocoon and finding a world of sunshine. Come on—' he started walking down the wharf again, tugging her along with him '—we're on our way there now.'

The first day of a new life…

Of course, that was how it had to be.

There was no point in looking back, mourning over foolish dreams that were never going to come true. She had to put Michael behind her. Lucy would still be there along the track, her episode with Michael gone and forgotten, flitting along in her usual ditzy way. Her sister would always be her sister. It was she who had to start a different journey and being sour about it was just going to hold her back from getting somewhere good.

Harry helped her onto a large, deep-sea fishing yacht, which undoubtedly had powerful motors to get them to their destination fast. 'Do you get seasick, Elizabeth?' he asked as he released the mooring rope. 'There are pills in the cabin you can take for it.'

'No, I'll be fine,' she assured him.

'I need you to be in top form when we arrive.'

'What do you consider top form?' She needed to know, get it right.

He jumped on board, grinning at her as he stored the rope correctly. 'Your usual self. Totally in charge of everything around you and projecting that haughty confidence you do so well.'

'Haughty?' she queried, not liking that description of herself, either.

'You're brilliant at it. Subject me to it every time.'

Only because Harry was Harry. It was her defence against him.

'I want you to give our target a dose of it when we confront him. No chatter. Just freeze him off.'

'No problem,' she stated categorically.

He straightened up and headed for the ladder to the bridge, tapping her cheek in passing, his eyes twinkling as he said, 'That's my girl!'

She barely stopped her hand from clapping her cheek to rid it of his electric touch. She clenched it into a fist and swiftly decided there would have to be some rules made about this short-term job on the island—like no touching from Harry. No kissing on the cheek, either. He was altogether too cavalier about taking liberties with her.

She was his stand-in manager, *not his girl*!

She was never going to be *his girl*.

One Finn brother had taken a bite out of her life. She was not about to give Harry the chance to take another. A month was a month. That was it with the Finns. She was thirty years old. When she'd completed this escape phase, some serious steps would have to be planned to make the best of the rest of her life.

She needed to find herself a serious man to share all that could be shared.

There was no hope of that happening with a playboy like Harry.

'Think you can make us both a sobering coffee while I fire up the engines?' he tossed back at her from the ladder.

'Sure! Though I'm not the least bit intoxicated, Harry.' She'd sobered up over lunch.

He grinned at her. 'I am. A straight black would be good. Join me on the bridge when you've made it.'

'Okay.'

She wanted to be fully briefed on the situation she was walking into, and Harry certainly needed to be fully in command of himself before they reached the island. Not that she'd noticed any lack of command. In fact, he'd been quite masterful in manipulating Michael into complying with what he wanted. She would have to watch that particular skill of his and not fall victim to any manipulation that would end up with her in the playboy's bed!

CHAPTER FIVE

EXHILARATION bubbled through Harry's brain. Who would have thought when today had started out that he would be riding towards the end of it on this glorious high? Here he was on the open sea, carving through the waves, the problem with his thieving manager solved, and the deliciously challenging Elizabeth at his beck and call for at least a month.

Her brick wall against him was still in place, but that blind obsession of hers with Mickey was gone. Lovely, lovely Lucy had done the job, blitzing his brother right in front of her sister's eyes. And at the most opportune moment! So easy to step in and take advantage of Elizabeth's disillusioned state.

She'd found herself trapped in a situation where pride had forced her to side with him, undoubtedly kicking and screaming about it in her mind, but totally unable to disguise the fact that she reacted to him physically. Always had. She could deny it as much as she liked but sexual chemistry didn't lie, and now that Mickey was out of the picture, cultivating the instinctive attraction she couldn't quite control was going to be the most enjoyable task Harry had set himself for some time.

Ellie Flippence...

That's who she needed to be, not stiff-necked Elizabeth. Though she did have a lovely long neck. He'd often fantasised bending that swanlike column with a trail of hot kisses, melting the rest of her, too. She had beautiful lush breasts and the gorgeous butterfly wings on her blouse showed them off a treat.

This morning he'd wanted to reach out and touch them, cup them, kiss them. He'd find the right time and place for that now. The moment would come when she'd give in to good old healthy lust, and Harry intended to make it so good she'd forget all about her shattered Mickey dreams and revel in the pleasure he'd give her.

But business came first.

He definitely needed to sober up, not give away the game before Elizabeth was ready for it.

Just as well she'd worn sandals, Elizabeth thought as she moved around the galley, steadying herself to the sway of the yacht as it headed out to sea. High heels would have been disastrous in this environment. Clearly there were tricks to keeping everything safe on board. She found a drink holder attached to a sling which made transporting coffee to the bridge relatively easy, and mugs with lids like the takeaway variety used by coffee shops. There was no risk of slopping it onto her good clothes which had to last her until her luggage arrived.

A scene flashed into her mind of Lucy in their apartment, with Michael advising her on what to choose for her sister's island wear—an intimate little scene that made Elizabeth gnash her teeth. She had to stop thinking of *them* together, think about what was ahead of her instead.

Finn Island was at the high end of the tourist industry—exclusive to only twenty couples at a time, people who could pay thousands of dollars for a minimum three-

day stay. She had never been there, since it
was way beyond her pocket. However, the
Cairns office did have a video of it, showing its attractions and facilities, so she had
some idea of how it operated.

There were twenty luxury villas, a tennis
court, a gym with a pampering centre offer-
ing all sorts of massages. The administration
centre, boutique, restaurant and bar faced the
main beach and were spread around a land-
scaped area with lush tropical plants and
clusters of palm trees, plus a swimming pool
and spa. Apart from this artfully designed
section, most of the island was covered with
rainforest. A creek running from the central
hill provided delightful waterfalls and rock
pools, and walking tracks had been made to
these natural beauty spots.

Dive-boats for exploring the Great Barrier
Reef were readily available, as were yachts
for deep-sea fishing and small motorboats for
reaching the other beaches at the various in-
lets around the shoreline. All in all, Finn Island provided the perfect tropical getaway…
if you were rolling in money.

Guests who could afford it would obviously be demanding, expecting the best for
what they were paying. Elizabeth hoped

there would be no hiccups to the island's excellent reputation for providing it while she was in charge. She knew supply boats called regularly. However, how the staff operated was a mystery to her and the need for that information was foremost in her mind as she climbed the ladder to the bridge.

She sat down in the chair beside Harry's before handing him his coffee. 'Black, as requested,' she said, forcing a smile to disprove his *sourpuss* description and holding on to a fierce determination not to be prickly in his presence.

'Thanks.' He smiled back. 'We'll be there in about forty minutes.'

'I know the general layout of the resort, but I know nothing about the staff, Harry. Or how everything runs.'

'You'll learn fast enough,' he assured her. 'Basically you have three undermanagers. Sarah Pickard is the head housekeeper. She handles the cleaning staff. Her husband, Jack, is the head maintenance man, who has his own team of helpers. The head chef, Daniel Marven, runs everything to do with the restaurant. He also keeps a check on the bar and will tell you what needs to be ordered in.' He made a wry grimace. 'The guy you

are going to replace was overordering and re-
selling elsewhere, not to mention a few other
perks he was working.'

'His name?'

'Sean Cassidy. Not important for you to
remember. He'll be gone within an hour of
our arrival. I'll call up a helicopter to take
him off.'

'Are you going to prosecute?'

He shook his head. 'Bad publicity. Besides, it wasn't major criminal stuff.'

'How did you find out he was crooked?'

'Our sommelier in Cairns remarked to me
that our island guests drank an inordinate
amount of wine and spirits. Surprisingly inordinate, despite the fact that we run an open
bar. It rang warning bells. When Sean had
his mainland leave this past weekend, I did a
thorough check of all supplies and usage, and
bingo! No doubt he was robbing us and has
been doing it for some considerable time.'

'Will he know you were checking on him?'

'He knows I was there but I didn't tip my
hand to anyone. Mickey and I still had to decide what to do about it. Any disruption is
not good for business.' He flashed a grin at
her. 'Which is where you come in. No disruption.'

She nodded. 'I'll do my best to make it appear a smooth transition, but I'll need some help to begin with.'

'No problem. I'll be your guide for the first few days, until you've familiarised yourself with how everything runs.'

A few days in close contact with Harry had to be tolerated. The groundwork for this management job had to be laid if she was to carry it through successfully. It was the measure of closeness she had to watch. If he started taking liberties with her person… somehow she had to deal with that if and when it happened.

'I'll get on top of it all as soon as I can,' she said with strong resolution.

Harry chuckled, his vivid blue eyes dancing with teasing knowledge as he slowly drawled, 'I'm sure you will, Elizabeth. Can't get rid of me fast enough, can you?'

She felt heat rushing up her neck and turned her face away, looking out to sea, hating how he could read her mind and provoke this reaction in her. 'I'm sure you have to keep a check on other things besides the resort,' she said flatly.

'True. Though I am aware that I'm throwing you into a position you haven't held before. I'll spend a few days with you, then drop in from time to time in case you have any problems that I can resolve.'

She wished she could say, *Don't. I'll call you if I need your help.* But he was her boss now and what he was laying out was reasonable. Problems could arise that she didn't even recognise because of her inexperience. 'Do you have accommodation kept especially for you on the island?' she asked, worrying about how *close* he was going to be to her.

'No. I'm happy sleeping aboard this yacht. The Pickards have their own private villa as they are the only ones on the staff, apart from the manager, who actually live on the island full-time. The rest work on a rotation basis—ten days here, four days on the mainland—and they're accommodated in a series of motel-like structures.'

'Is that where I'll be staying?'

He shook his head. 'You'll have your own private quarters in the administration building.'

Where Harry could make private visits.

Elizabeth grimaced at that thought. She was getting paranoid about the man. He could not get her into bed with him unless she allowed it. All she had to do was keep him at a sensible distance. It was only for a month and he wouldn't be there all the time.

'Don't be worrying about clothes for to-morrow,' he suddenly tossed at her. 'I'll get Sarah to issue you with the island uniform.'

'What's the island uniform?' she queried, not having seen that on the video.

'This…' He indicated his T-shirt and shorts and pointed to the emblem just below his left shoulder—a stitched line of waves in blue over which *Finn Island* was written in a small flowing multicoloured script to match the multicoloured fish across his chest.

She hadn't noticed the emblem before, distracted by the way the T-shirt clung to Harry's very male physique. 'I hadn't realised. Of course, you came from there this morning.'

So much had happened today, her state of hopeful eagerness this morning felt as though it had been wiped out a million years ago. Another life ago.

'Makes it easier for the guests to know who's staff and who's not,' Harry explained, adding with one of his devilish grins, 'That won't take care of your undies, though.'

He was probably having a fantasy of her naked beneath her outer clothes.

'I'll manage,' she said through gritted teeth.

He laughed. 'You can probably pick up a bikini from the boutique. Sarah can provide you with a hair-dryer and a toothbrush. Don't know about make-up.'

'I have some in my handbag.'

'No worries then.'

Only you, she thought.

Yet when they arrived on the island and confronted Sean Cassidy in his administration office, the playboy image Elizabeth had of Harry Finn in her mind was severely dented. Right in front of her eyes his easy-going attitude disappeared, replaced by a formidable air of authority. There was no semblance of light banter in his voice as he set about firing the crooked manager with ruthless efficiency.

Sean Cassidy had risen from the chair behind his office desk to greet his visitors, a smile on his face that didn't quite reach his eyes, which skated over Elizabeth and settled warily on Harry. He was a tall, lean man, dark-haired, dark-eyed, and the unheralded appearance of his boss clearly caused some tension in him.

'You're out, Sean,' Harry shot at him before the manager could say a word. 'Move away from the desk. Don't touch anything in this office. A helicopter will be arriving shortly to fly you to the mainland. Go and collect all your personal effects from your apartment. You won't be coming back.'

'What the hell…' the guy started to expostulate.

Harry cut him off. 'You know why. I have evidence of all your skimming activities. Providing you go quietly, I won't hand you over to the police at this time. If you know what's good for you, Sean, you'll stay quiet. Any bad-mouthing of the Finn family and its business operations will have consequences you won't like. Do you understand me?'

The threat had a steely edge to it that would have intimidated anyone. Sean Cassidy sucked in his breath, swallowed whatever defensive words he might have spoken and nodded. He looked shell-shocked.

'Let's go then.' Harry waved commandingly to a door in the rear wall of the office. 'I'll accompany you into the apartment to ensure you don't take anything that doesn't belong to you.'

As the man started to move as directed, Harry turned to Elizabeth, his blue eyes ice-hard, not a vestige of a twinkle in them.

'Take over the desk, Elizabeth. You're now in charge of this office.'

She nodded, her mouth too dry to speak. Her heart was beating faster than normal. The air felt charged with electricity. She was still stunned by the strike-anyone-dead energy that had emanated from Harry. In her two years of working for Michael, she had never witnessed anything like it coming from him, and she had always thought he was the stronger brother.

It wasn't until Harry had followed Sean into the apartment and closed the door that she could bring herself to actually move her feet. The desk was large and L-shaped with a computer workstation on one side. She sat in the chair that was now hers, grateful for its firm support. Witnessing the formidable side of Harry Finn had shaken her. The man was lethal, and she suddenly felt very vulnerable to whatever he might turn on her, now that she was locked into this situation with him.

That nerve-quivering blast of forcefulness... A shiver ran down her spine. Though surely he would never *force* a woman. *He wouldn't have to*, came the instant answer in her head. He was so innately sexy he could make her feel hot and bothered with just a teasing look. But he needed her here for business so maybe he would refrain from pushing anything sexual with her. Teasing was just teasing. Hopefully she could keep a level head with that.

Having cleared her mind enough to concentrate on business, Elizabeth took stock of the other office furnishings—filing cabinets, a couple of chairs for visitors, a coffee table with brochures fanned out on top of it, framed photographs of celebrities who had stayed here hanging on the walls.

On the larger section of the desk, which faced the entrance doors to administration, was a telephone attached to an intercom system with numbers for all the villas, the staff quarters and the restaurant. Beside it was a notepad and pen for writing notes or messages. On the top page were two reminders which had been ticked. *Chocs to 8. Gin to 14.* Obviously she had to deal with all requests from guests as well as handle bookings and coordinate the staff for whatever was needed.

Directly in front of her was a spreadsheet, detailing the occupancy of the villas this week—arrivals and departures. Three couples had left this morning. Their villas were vacant until another three couples ar-

rived tomorrow. One of them was only staying three days, the other two for five. Most
of the bookings were for five, only a few
for a whole week. She would have to have
her wits about her, coordinating the turn-
overs, personalising the welcomes and the
farewells, memorising the names of all the
guests. Wealthy people always expected that
courtesy and respect.

She was matching names to the occupants
of each villa when she heard the distinctive
sound of a helicopter coming in. The door
behind her opened and Harry led Sean, who
was loaded up with luggage, out of the apartment, waving him to go ahead, pausing at
the desk long enough to say, 'Hold the fort,
Elizabeth. I'll be back in twenty minutes.'

He didn't wait for a reply, intent on es-
corting Sean to the helipad, wherever that
was. The glass entrance doors to the office
opened automatically for ease of access and
Harry caught up with Sean as he made his
exit. There was no verbal exchange between
them. The ex-manager was going quietly.

Elizabeth watched Harry until he moved
out of sight. Her heart was hammering again.
Experiencing a completely different side of
Harry Finn to the flirtatious tease she was

used to was having a highly disturbing impact on her. It was impossible now to dismiss him as a lightweight playboy. The man had real substance, impressively strong substance, powerful substance, and it was playing havoc with her prejudice against him.

Michael had said this morning that Harry's mind was as sharp as a razor blade and he had his thumb on everything to do with his side of the business. That description could no longer be doubted. She'd had evidence enough today of how accurately he could read her thoughts—something she would have to guard against more carefully in the future—and she would never again underestimate how capable he was of being master of any situation.

His attraction was all the stronger for it. Dangerously so.

Nevertheless, that still didn't make him good relationship material.

He was a dyed-in-the-wool flirt with women.

And that wasn't just her judgment. Michael had said so.

Regardless of what Harry Finn made her feel, she was not going to have anything to do with him apart from the business of managing this resort for a month. He could flirt

his head off with her but she would stand absolutely firm on that ground.

He was not what she wanted in her life.

She had to look for someone steady, solid,
totally committed to her and the family they
would have together.

Not like her father.

And not like Harry, who probably treated
women as though they were a carousel of
lollipops to be plucked out and tasted until
another looked tastier.

CHAPTER SIX

WHEN Harry returned he was accompanied by a middle-aged woman with whom he appeared to be on very friendly terms. They were smiling at each other as they entered the office. She had short, curly dark hair, liberally streaked with grey, a very attractive face set in cheerful lines and merry hazel eyes that invited people to enjoy life with her. Of average height, her trim figure declared her fit to tackle anything, and she exuded positive vibes at Elizabeth as Harry introduced her.

'Sarah Pickard, Elizabeth.'

'Hi! Welcome to Finn Island,' the woman chimed in.

'Thank you.' Elizabeth smiled back as she rose from the desk to offer her hand at this first meeting. 'I'll have to learn a lot very fast and I'll appreciate any help and advice you can give me, Sarah.'

She laughed and gave Elizabeth's hand a quick squeeze. 'No problem. I'm only ever a call away. Harry tells me you've been Mickey's PA. I'm sure you'll fit in here very quickly.'

Mickey? The familiar use of Harry's name for his brother struck her as odd.

'Go into the apartment with Sarah, look around, see what you need,' Harry instructed. 'I'll man the desk.'

'Okay. Thank you,' Elizabeth replied, gesturing to Sarah to lead the way.

It was a basic one-bedroom apartment, spotlessly clean and pleasantly furnished with cane furniture, cushions brightly patterned in tropical designs. The floor was tiled and an airconditioner kept the rooms cool. The kitchenette was small, and its only equipment appeared to be an electric kettle, a toaster and a microwave oven.

'You won't need that for much,' Sarah explained. 'Meals will be brought to you from the restaurant. Just tick what you want on each menu. You'll find tea, coffee and sugar in the cupboard above the sink, milk and cold drinks in the bar fridge.'

Elizabeth nodded, thinking the gourmet meals provided here were a wonderful perk—no shopping for food, no cooking and no cleaning up afterwards.

'The bed linen was changed this morning so everything's fresh for you apart from these towels.' Which she'd collected from the bathroom as she'd showed Elizabeth the facilities. 'I'll send clean ones over for you. Plus a hair-dryer and toothbrush. Harry said he'd whipped you off Mickey with no time to pack anything.'

Again the familiar name usage. Elizabeth frowned quizzically. 'He's always been Michael to me. I've only heard Harry calling him Mickey. And now you.'

She laughed. 'I've known those two since they were teenagers. Jack and I looked after their parents' place in those days. I guess I was like a second mother to them. Never had kids of my own. Good boys, both of them. You couldn't be connected to better men, Elizabeth, as employers or people.'

It was a high recommendation, though probably a biased one, given Sarah's obvious fondness for them. 'They're very different,' she commented, wanting to hear more.

'Mickey's more like his dad, a seriously

driven achiever. It's in his genes, I reckon. Harry's nature is more like his mum's. She had a very sunny disposition, radiating a joy in life that infected everyone around her. It was a wicked shame when...' She heaved a deep sigh. 'Well, I guess we never know the day or the hour, but I tell you, those boys are a credit to their parents. Losing them both when they did, they could have run off the rails, plenty of money to spend, but they took on the business and pushed forward. And they looked after everyone who could have been hurt by the loss. Like me and Jack.'

She paused, grimaced. 'Here I am running off at the mouth but you know Mickey. Harry said you've been working closely with him for two years.'

'Yes, I have.'

'You'll find Harry good to work for, too. Just a different nature, that's all.'

Sunny...like his mother...like Lucy. Was that why Michael was so attracted to Lucy? But why wasn't Harry? Why did he have to plague her with his endlessly provocative attention?

'I'll only be here for a month, Sarah. I'm the fill-in until Harry finds a replacement for Sean.'

'Whatever...' She waved airily. Obviously it was not something that weighed on her mind. 'I'll send over sets of the island uniform with the towels etc. Do you want short shorts, Bermuda length or three-quarters?'

'Bermuda length,' Elizabeth decided, thinking that would look more dignified for her position as manager.

'Harry thought a bikini...?'

'No. I'll wash my undies out tonight. I'll be fine, thanks, Sarah.'

She grinned. 'I love your butterfly blouse. It's just the kind of thing Harry's mum used to wear.'

Lucy's choice, Elizabeth thought. 'I'll gladly change it for tropical fish,' she said. The butterfly blouse represented failure with Michael and trouble with Harry, since he saw it as sexy. 'I'll be more comfortable here in the island uniform.'

'Well, it is easy. You don't have to think about what clothes to put on. I'll be off now. You might want to freshen up before rejoining Harry in the office.'

'Yes, I do. Thanks, Sarah.'

She was relieved to have such a good ally in the head housekeeper. It would surely make this job easier. Sarah's long association with the Finn family meant that she could be absolutely trusted, too.

What she'd said about *the two boys* lingered in Elizabeth's mind as she made use of the bathroom facilities. The plane crash that had taken the lives of Franklyn and Yvette Finn had been frontline news about ten years ago, soon after her own mother had died. She hadn't known the people so it had meant nothing personal to her at the time, yet it must have been a traumatic period for Michael and Harry, both young men, possibly still at university, having fun, believing there was plenty of time to work out what they wanted to do with their lives. It *was* admirable that they'd taken on their father's business empire instead of selling up and shedding all responsibility.

But it still didn't make Harry good relationship material. She could respect him for what he'd done. He might be very *solid* in that sense. However, that did not mean he had any staying power where women were concerned.

For the next hour she had to sit beside him at the computer workstation in the office while he went through the Finn Island website, showing her how bookings were made over the internet and their dates subsequently slotted into the island calendar. He explained how to work out all the schedules that had to be kept and Elizabeth had no trouble grasping what she had to do.

However, being so close to Harry—virtually shoulder to shoulder—did make concentration more difficult than it should have been. With their brief encounters in the Cairns office, she'd always managed to keep her distance from him, hating how he could exude a male sexiness that made her acutely conscious of being a woman whose needs weren't being answered. Now, having barely any space between them made her senses hyperalert to almost everything about him.

Her nose kept being invaded by his smell—a sharp tanginess like a sea breeze somehow mixed with an earthy animal scent. His strong, muscular forearms were a very masculine contrast to her more slender, softly rounded ones and she couldn't help noticing his long dexterous fingers as he worked the computer mouse—fingers that fascinated her into flights of erotic fantasy. He didn't touch her, not even accidentally, but she was wound up inside, expecting him to, silently schooling herself not to react as though his touch was like a hot iron scorching her skin.

She had to learn how to behave naturally around him. Whenever he glanced at her to check if she understood what he was explaining, the vivid blue eyes seemed to be tunnelling into her mind and she had to force herself to hold his gaze as she assured him everything was clear to her. Then he smiled approval which made her stupid stomach contract. He was an extremely disturbing man even when he wasn't teasing or flirting and she didn't want him to be. Hopefully his wretchedly unsettling effect on her would gradually fade away over the next few days.

People started strolling by on the path outside, heading towards the bar for predinner drinks. Harry named them as they passed. Of course he had been here over this past weekend, but it was impressive that he could identify every guest on the island and tell her where they came from, as well as how they'd come by their wealth. Elizabeth tried to commit most of what he said to memory but it was a struggle—too many of them, too quickly.

'You'll soon have them down pat,' Harry said confidently. 'I told Daniel we'd be eating in the restaurant tonight. I'll drill you on everyone at the other tables while we dine, then introduce you around before they leave.'

'That would help a lot,' she said gratefully.

'Hope you can find some more appetite than you had for lunch. Daniel will be miffed if you don't do justice to his gourmet creations.'

He knew she'd been too upset to eat much lunch but tonight she wouldn't have to watch Michael and Lucy gobbling up each other and she wanted to stop Harry from poking any further at the still-raw place in her heart. 'Actually I'm rather hungry. Must be the sea air,' she answered airily, resolving to eat everything put in front of her and show appreciation of it, regardless of how she *felt*.

His eyes glittered satisfaction. 'Remarkable what a sea change will do.'

Well, it won't extend to sharing your bed, she silently promised him as she rolled her chair back from the desk and stood up. 'Speaking of change, I'll go and swap these clothes for the island uniform before we go to the restaurant.'

Two young women on Sarah's staff—Maddie and Kate—had brought everything she needed while Harry had been teaching her the ins and outs of the website. The way they'd looked at Harry—telegraphing they thought he was *hot*—had made her wonder if he played musical beds on the island.

'Good idea!' He eyed her up and down in that lingering way that made her skin prickle. 'We wouldn't want our lady guests going pea-green with envy at how gorgeous you look in that outfit,' he drawled. 'Nor would we want their guys seeing you as more desirable than their partners.'

'Oh, really!' she huffed, crossing her arms defensively.

'Just telling you how it is, dear Elizabeth.'

'Don't *dear* me!' she snapped, still very much on edge from having to weather the sexual pitfalls of his proximity and wanting to cut off his flirting routine.

His eyebrows arched provocatively. 'What? I can't express how I feel about you?'

One of her hands sliced out in negative dismissal. 'I don't want to hear it.'

'Wrong time, wrong man, but that doesn't make it any less true.'

She rolled her eyes in disbelief. 'Let's keep to business, Harry.'

'Okay.' He gestured at the door to the apartment. 'Go and change. It will be a start to fitting in with me instead of Mickey.'

She felt purpose underlying those words, spine-crawling purpose as she turned her back on him and walked quickly from the office into the apartment, closing the door very firmly behind her.

It caused her to work up some steely purpose of her own. She would do her best to fit in on the island but fitting in with Harry on any personal basis had to stop. It had been a purely defensive move, going along with him today, using him as a shield to hide her distress. From now on she should take control of whatever happened between them. Her mind was very clear on that. She certainly didn't want to invite any sexual complications with him, which would only mess her around more than she was already messed up by the situation with Michael and Lucy.

It was a relief to shed the clothes that had fed her hopes this morning. She had a quick shower to wash away the misery of the day and give herself the sense of making a fresh start. It felt liberating donning the island uniform. This was the end of maintaining the professional image of an executive PA, at least for the next month. The casual, carefree look of shorts and T-shirt was suddenly very welcome to her.

It seemed she'd been carrying a heavy weight of responsibility for many years, ever since her mother had fallen ill with terminal cancer and her father had deserted them. The need to hold everything together for herself and Lucy had been driving her for a long time. Somehow it didn't matter so much anymore. She was on an island, away from the life she had known up until now, all by herself...except for Harry, who'd be gone as soon as she was on top of the job.

That was her main priority now—demonstrating to Harry that his guidance was no longer needed. Once she was free of his presence, this place might very well work some magic for her—time out of time to find herself again—no hanging on to what Michael thought or felt about her, no worrying about Lucy, just Elizabeth.

CHAPTER SEVEN

HARRY watched her come out of the apartment, all bright-eyed and bushy-tailed, determined to get on with the job and do it well. He admired her strength of character, her refusal to be utterly crushed by disillusionment. On the other hand, he had kept her mind very occupied these past few hours and would continue to do so until they parted for the night. That would be crunch time for her, when she was lying in bed, alone in the darkness. It would all be about Mickey and Lucy then.

He was strongly tempted to give her something else to think about—something she couldn't dismiss as easily as she had in the past, writing him off as of no account. He didn't like it. He never had liked it. Tonight might be too soon to pounce but...what the hell! She was never going to be *ready* for him. Her mind-set against getting personally involved with him was so fixed, perhaps physically shaking her out of it was the best way to go.

If he set the scene right...

An idea came to him. A private word to the chef before dinner, concentrate on business over the meal, wait until the guests had drifted off to their villas or the bar, then spring the surprise.

He grinned at her as he rose from the office chair. 'Time to see if the stars are burning bright tonight.'

She shook her head at him. 'It's not dark enough yet.' Her tone denied any interest in an activity which probably smacked of romance to her.

'Well, we can watch for them to appear from our table in the restaurant. You are allowed to enjoy the ambience of this island, Elizabeth.'

He could see her consciously relaxing, working up a smile. 'I will, Harry. I'm glad I have the opportunity to do so.'

'Good! I want you to be happy here.'

Happy...

Why not? Elizabeth thought. She should let everything else float out of her mind and embrace this experience—tropical night, stars burning bright, glorious food, lots of interesting people to meet. All she had to do was ignore Harry's insidious effect on her, and with the ready distraction of the guests around them, surely that could be kept at bay.

He led her out of the office, locked the doors and handed her the key, which made her feel secure about any unwanted attention coming from him later on in the evening. As soon as they entered the spacious, open-air restaurant, he was called over to a table where two couples were very happy with their day of diving near the reef, happy that Harry had arranged such a marvellous experience for them.

Elizabeth was introduced as the new manager. It was easy to smile at these people, easy to smile at all the other guests when other introductions were made throughout the evening. They were all having a great time and their mood was infectious, and however they'd filled in their day, the evening meal certainly topped it off.

Every course was superb. Elizabeth really enjoyed the food and complimented the chef on it, praising the attentiveness of the waiters, too. Daniel Marven definitely ran a high-class restaurant. Elizabeth couldn't see any problem arising on this front during her management month, and she was sure Sarah and Jack Pickard handled their roles just as efficiently. This could very well be a *happy* position for her.

'You have a great set-up here, Harry,' she complimented him over coffee. 'The guests are so clearly enjoying themselves.'

He leaned back in his chair, smiling at her. 'You've handled everything extremely well, Elizabeth.'

His voice was like a soft purr that somehow seemed to curl around her, adding more heat to the warmth of his smile. All evening it had been strictly business, with Harry coaching her in her managerial role, and she'd relaxed enough to actually feel comfortable with him. She was caught off guard by the switch to personal appreciation that felt as though he was physically caressing her.

Her pulse quickened. Her toes scrunched up in her sandals. He wasn't really *doing* anything, she fiercely told herself. It hadn't even been a flirtatious remark. Reacting like this was off the wall.

'Thank you,' she said quickly, fighting off the unwelcome feelings.

'No. Thank *you*,' he replied just as quickly, the smile gone, respect shining in his eyes. 'Coming in cold, taking over from Sean… you're picking up on everything much faster than I expected. This morning I had a problem. Tonight…' He spread his hands in an awed gesture. 'You're a wonder, Elizabeth.'

She floundered for a moment, his warmth and respect tearing at her heart—the heart she had given to Michael, who didn't want it. She made an ironic grimace. 'Your brother trained me to pick up on everything.'

He returned the grimace. 'Of course. Mickey would. But I'm glad you're here with me.'

And she was glad to have this getaway.

That was the bottom line.

She forced herself to relax again. Today was almost over. She'd made it through without falling apart.

As the last couple rose from their table to leave the restaurant they called out goodnights to Harry and Elizabeth, which, of course, they reciprocated. 'Colin and Jayne Melville from Goulburn,' Elizabeth murmured, shooting a triumphant grin at Harry. 'I've got them all sorted now.'

He laughed, the blue eyes twinkling plea-

sure in her. 'I knew you'd meet the challenge.'

Her heart did a flip-flop. The man was
sinfully attractive, actually more so when
he wasn't doing his playboy *flirting* stuff.
Tonight he hadn't strayed into any irritating
dalliance with her, focusing entirely on eas-
ing her into this new job. He'd been excep-
tionally good at it, too, charming the guests
into talking about themselves, giving information for Elizabeth to memorise. They enjoyed chatting with him. Of course, in their
eyes Harry Finn was an equal. He had the
money, the looks and the self-assurance that
came with both those assets.

'One more thing to do before we part for
the night,' he said, standing up and moving
to draw back her chair.

'What's that?' she asked, pushing herself
up from the table, feeling it had been a very
long day already.

'A little ceremony from the staff to welcome you,' he answered. 'It's been set up
down on the deck.' He nodded towards the
bar where many of the guests had gathered
for a nightcap. It was directly across from
the restaurant, the walkway down to the pool

deck dividing the two entertainment areas. 'More private than here.'

Elizabeth had no qualms about accompanying Harry to wherever the welcome ceremony was going to be held. It was a nice gesture from the staff and gave her the opportunity to meet more of them.

There were actually two decks. The first one surrounded the swimming pool. It was strewn with sun-lounges, tables with folded-up umbrellas, and a couple of day beds flanking it. Steps led down to a lower deck, which had a large spa to one side.

A table for two was set up just in front of more steps that led straight onto the beach; white tablecloth, an ice bucket containing a bottle of champagne, two flute glasses, two bread plates with cake forks beside them. *A table for two*, in what was so obviously a romantic setting, close to the sound of waves lapping on the beach and under a sky full of stars.

Elizabeth jolted to a halt. Her pulse jumped into an erratic beat. This looked too much like a playboy setting. Was Harry about to turn into a wolf now that business was over for the day? She shot him a hard, suspicious look.

'I don't see any staff.'

'Waiting for me to get you settled,' he said, moving ahead to hold out one of the chairs for her.

Was it true? Surely he wouldn't lie when the lie could be so quickly disproved. It was okay, she told herself, taking a deep breath and letting it out slowly as she forced her feet forward and sat where Harry had directed. He lifted the bottle of champagne out of the ice bucket, popped the cork and filled the flute glasses before sitting down himself.

'A celebratory drink,' he said, smiling at her as he raised his glass, expecting her to do the same.

She did, though his smile did nothing to calm her down. Quite the opposite.

'To a new start,' he added, clicking her glass with his.

'A new start,' she echoed, hoping the staff would hurry up and appear. Her nerves were twitching. Her heart was thumping. There was too much intimacy about being alone with Harry out here, and the control she was trying to hold on to was frayed by having had to deal with too many difficult situations.

Harry's eyes caressed her with admiration as he complimented her again. 'You've been brilliant today, Elizabeth.'

For some stupid reason, tears pricked her eyes. She managed a half smile of acknowledgment and quickly sipped the champagne, needing it to loosen up the sudden lump in her throat. The day had been overloaded with tensions but it was almost over. All she had to do was hold herself together a little bit longer.

'Ah! Here it comes!' Harry said happily, looking up towards the restaurant.

Elizabeth blinked hard, set her glass down, mentally gathered herself to deal with the welcome ceremony, then turned her head to see…

Not a group of staff members.

Only one person walking down the steps.

It was Daniel Marven, carrying a cake on a platter.

She looked for others to come streaming down behind him but no one did. He proceeded to the table alone, placing the platter in front of her.

'Enjoy,' he said, smiling at her.

Happy Birthday Elizabeth was written across the chocolate icing on top of the cake. She stared at it, barely finding voice enough to say, 'Thank you.'

'Good work, Daniel,' Harry said, and the

chef took off, leaving the two of them to-gether.

A dam of tightly held emotion burst inside Elizabeth. Her birthday. Her thirtieth birth-day. She'd so much wanted it to be…not how it had turned out. Tears spurted into her eyes, welling over and streaming down her cheeks. Impossible to stop them. Her heart was not strong enough to absorb any more stress. It felt as though it was breaking.

Strong hands lifted her out of her chair. Strong arms engulfed her, clamping her to a strong chest. Her head was gently pressed onto a strong shoulder. There was no resis-tance in her. None at all. She was as weak as a baby—a baby who had been born thirty years ago and didn't know what life had in store for her. Still didn't. And she was too much at sea to think about it…think about anything.

CHAPTER EIGHT

HARRY had not anticipated having a weeping Elizabeth in his arms. The birthday cake surprise had been planned to give her pleasure and undermine her resistance to a friendly goodnight kiss, which could have easily escalated into something more, sparking up the chemistry that she'd always been so determined to deny. He didn't feel right about taking advantage of *this* situation.

What had caused such deep distress? Was it the reminder that she had turned thirty today? Single women could be rather touchy about reaching that age goalpost, particularly if they weren't in a relationship and wanted to be. Was it the lost chance with Mickey catching up with her at the end of the day?

It was so damnably frustrating. He'd finally got her to himself. She felt good in his arms—all woman—soft, warm and curvy.

Smelled good, too. He rubbed his cheek over her hair, breathing in the scent of her——a fruity shampoo and an enticing trace of exotic perfume. He patted her back, trying to impart comfort, and felt relieved when the weeping started trailing off, interrupted by deep, heaving breaths that made him very aware of the lush fullness of her breasts. He wanted to pick her up, carry her over to the nearest day bed and blow her mind with wild, passionate sex.

The emotional storm eventually came to a shuddering halt but she remained leaning on him, her head resting on his shoulder, her body still, limp, spent of all energy. His hands wanted to wander, travelling down the very female curve of her spine to her even more female bottom——the bottom that swished provocatively every time she'd turned away from him. His fingers itched to curl around it, press her body into a more intimate fit with his, stir the same desire in her that was heating up his blood, arousing the beast.

He couldn't stop himself from hardening, didn't want to anyway. Let her feel what she did to him. Let her know she was desirable even as a limp, tear-soaked rag doll. It might jolt her out of whatever sea of misery she was swimming in. Life was for living, not wallowing in a trough of depression.

Elizabeth didn't care that it was Harry holding her. It was simply nice to be held in such a secure comforting way, propping her up when she was down, not asking anything of her, just being another body emanating warmth that took the chill of loneliness from her bones.

She wished she had someone who would always be there for her like this, someone strong who would never let her down. She'd wanted to believe it would be Michael, but it wasn't. And Harry…oh hell! She could feel him getting hard! No matter that she'd been weeping all over him. He still had sex on his mind.

A flood of embarrassment poured heat into her face as she jerked her head up from his shoulder. She'd been hanging on to him like a limpet. It took a moment to unglue her hands from his back and try shoving them up his chest to make some space between them.

'Sorry…sorry,' she gabbled, frantically looking up to beg his understanding that she hadn't been passively inviting *anything*!

'Sorry for what?' he mocked, his eyes glittering a hard challenge at her.

'I didn't mean to…to use you like that.'

'You needed to…just like I need to do this.'

He whipped up a hand to hold her chin. Elizabeth didn't have time to protest, nor time to take any action to stop his mouth from swooping on hers. The impact shocked her. It was not a gentle seductive kiss. It was a full-on sensual assault, his lips working over hers, forcing them open with the strong thrust of his tongue that instantly swept over her palate, causing her whole mouth to tingle as though it had been charged with electricity.

Instinctively she used her own tongue to fight the invasion of his, angry at his bold aggression. Whether he took this as encouragement or not, she didn't know, but his hand moved to the back of her head, fingers thrusting into her hair, holding her so there was no escape from his marauding mouth. His tongue was teasing, goading, enticing hers to tangle erotically with it, resulting in an explosion of sensation that tore any sensible thoughts out of her mind.

The whole physicality of the moment was totally overwhelming. She didn't care that he pressed her lower body so closely to his that his erection furrowed her stomach. Some primitive part of her revelled in it, revelled in the hot hard wall of his chest squashing her breasts. She was swamped by a tidal wave of chaotic need to feel everything more and more intensely. Her own hands raked down his beautifully muscled back and curled around his taut male butt, exulting in the sense of taking this incredibly sexy man as hers.

It was wildly exciting, intoxicating—one avid kiss merging into another and another, inciting a fever of passion that possessed her with such power she completely lost herself in it, craving the fierce climactic union they were driving towards, the desire for it sweeping through her like a firestorm, all-consuming.

The mouth engaging hers suddenly broke the primal connection. 'Yes…' hissed into her ear—a sound of exultant triumph. Then the intimate body contact was shifted. Her legs were hoisted up and she was being carried with heart-pounding speed, cool air wafting over her hot face, reducing the fever of urgently demanding desire.

She was tumbled onto a bed and Harry—

Harry!—was leaping onto it to join her there. Her eyes were wide-open now. Her mind crashed into working gear. This was one of the day beds on the deck. She'd wanted the sex that Harry was intent on having with her. Her body was still quivering at a peak of need for it. But it was madness to go on with it—madness to muddy up what should be a clean break away from everything, starting what would inevitably be a messy affair going nowhere and interfering with carrying through this management job.

He flung one strongly muscled thigh over hers and started lifting her T-shirt as he lowered his head to start kissing her again. She'd lain inert with shock at finding herself so complicit in stirring this situation. It had to be stopped. Now! Already his hand was on her breast, fingers moving under the cup of her bra, tweaking her nipple, and for a moment she was paralysed by a rebellious wish to feel more of his touch. She stared at his mouth coming closer and closer, her mind screaming that another kiss would tip her over into Harry's world.

Did she want that?

Did she?

Losing control of everything?

A flash of fear whipped her hand up to Harry's mouth, covering it just before it made contact with hers. His eyebrows beetled down in a puzzled frown.

'Stop!' she croaked.

He jerked his head back from her halting hand, his frown deepening as he shot a disbelieving 'What?' at her.

She swallowed hard to give her voice more strength. 'I don't want you to take this any further, Harry.'

'Why not?' he demanded. 'You want it as much as I do.'

She wrenched his hand away from her breast and pulled the T-shirt down. 'A momentary madness,' she excused.

'Rubbish! It's been simmering between us for years,' he insisted vehemently. 'It just came to a head and it's damned dishonest of you to back off now.'

Anger stirred. She hadn't really consented to this. He'd started it when she was at her weakest, taking advantage of her vulnerable state. 'I don't care what you call it, I don't choose to go on with it,' she said fiercely and attempted to roll away from him.

He scooped her back to face him, his eyes blazing furious frustration. 'What is the matter with you? We want each other. It's only natural to…'

'Let me go, Harry. This isn't right for me.'

'Not right?' he repeated incredulously. 'It sure as hell felt right until you suddenly decided it wasn't, but I'm not into forcing any woman to have sex with me.' He threw up the arm that had halted her rejection of any more togetherness. 'If you hadn't responded as you did…'

'I didn't mean to,' she yelled at him, her face flaming at the truth he was flinging at her.

'Oh, yes you did! Just for once you let that steel-trap mind of yours open enough for your instincts to take over and it was dynamite between us. Is that what scares you, Elizabeth?'

She hated how he could always hit the nail on the head with her. Yes, it scared her but she wasn't going to admit it. She glared resentment at him. 'I figure you're dynamite to a lot of women, Harry, and I don't care to be left in little pieces when you move on to your next piece of fluff.'

His hand sliced the air in savage dismissal of her argument. 'I don't think of you as *fluff*! Do you imagine I'd give this management job to someone I thought of as *fluff*?'

'I'm not saying you didn't believe I could do the work. But having a bit of sex on the side was on the plate, too, wasn't it?' she hurled back at him. 'And now you're peeved because I've decided not to cooperate.'

He rolled his head in exasperation. 'Peeved does not describe what I feel right now, Elizabeth.'

There was a mountain of feeling brooding behind those words and Elizabeth instantly felt threatened by it. She scrambled off the day bed, swinging around on her feet to face down any follow-up from Harry. He hadn't moved. He lay sprawled across the bed with his head propped up on his hand, his eyes searing hers with blistering accusation.

'You're shutting the gate on living life to the full,' he said bitingly. 'I don't want your cooperation, Elizabeth. I want your surrender to what we could have together.'

'That's not the life I want,' she retorted decisively.

'You're chasing dreams instead of taking on what's real.'

'*My* choice.'

'One I can't respect,' he mocked.

'I won't stay here unless you do, Harry.'

'Oh, I will on the surface, Elizabeth. You need have no fear of any unwelcomed advances from me. It will be strictly business tomorrow and any other day I'm here.'

She should have felt relieved, but there was an aching heaviness in her stomach, a drag of physical disappointment that was not about to be easily shifted. 'In that case I'll stay,' she said flatly. Where else could she go and not be faced with Michael and Lucy? One thing she could certainly say for Harry—he had the knack of blotting them out for a while.

'Your call.' His mouth took on an ironic twist as he added, 'And do feel free to call on me if you decide to change your mind and explore a different kind of life to the one you've planned so rigidly.'

She took a deep breath to ease the tightness in her chest and said, 'Well, I'm glad we have that sorted.'

'Yes, you're a regular sorting machine, Elizabeth, everything slotted into its proper place,' he drawled as he rolled off the other side of the day bed and faced her across it. 'One day you might find there's pleasure in improper activities.'

'Not today,' she said through gritted teeth,

determined not to be taunted into doing anything reckless and stupid.

'No, not today,' he agreed mockingly. 'I take it you're about to say goodnight?'

'Yes.'

'I'll fetch your cake. I wouldn't want you to go without comfort food in the lonely darkness of the night.'

The cake.

She had completely forgotten it.

Wanted to forget it now but she couldn't, not with the chef having made it especially for her. She would have to eat some of it, too, show appreciation.

Harry strode down the steps to the table that had been set for them. At his orders. She was sure of that. Hoping to sweeten her up to the point where he would slide into making a move on her. Her stomach curdled at how easy she had made it for him, and how quickly she had been caught up in the dynamic sexuality he could put out at will.

Her thighs were aquiver from having been in such intimate contact with him and her breasts were still in a state of arousal. He had excited her—almost to the point of no return—and he could probably do it again if she let him. Would he keep his word—

strictly business from now on unless she gave him the green light?

He picked up the cake platter. Elizabeth realised she hadn't even moved from where she'd scrambled off the day bed. If Harry saw her still standing beside it he might think she regretted her decision. She jerked into walking, rounding the bed and heading up towards the administration office.

Harry had given her the door key after he had locked up before dinner. She dug it out of her shorts pocket, anxious to have the door open and be standing right there, ready to receive the cake from him so he had no reason to come in with it. Being alone with him in any enclosed space right now would severely stretch nerves that were already wildly agitated at having to be face to face with him, just for a few moments.

It surprised her to see guests laughing and chatting in the open bar lounge as she passed by. It had seemed so *private* on the lower decks. What if any of these people had strolled down to the beach while she and Harry… It didn't bear thinking about. Reckless, shameless…her face flamed at how very nearly she had succumbed to almost a *public* sex act.

Anger simmered as she unlocked the door, opened it and turned to take the cake platter from Harry, who had virtually caught up with her. 'Did you realise there were still people up and about when you swept me off to that bed?' she demanded accusingly.

'So what?' He arched his eyebrows at her as though she was mad.

'Oh, you don't care about anything, do you?' she cried in exasperation and tried to snatch the platter from him.

He held on to it, forcing her to meet his gaze, a blast of hot resentment burning over her own. 'On the contrary, I care about a lot of things, Elizabeth. As to your quite unnecessary embarrassment at the thought of being observed in flagrante, this happens to be a tropical island where people drop their inhibitions and feel free to have sex wherever and whenever they want it. Using that bed under the stars for some natural pleasure in the privacy of the night would not offend anyone.'

'I'm not a guest. I'm staff,' she argued furiously.

His chin jutted with arrogant authority. 'This island is mine. I can make any rules I like for whomever I like.'

'I live by my own rules, Harry,' she flared

at him. 'Now let me have the cake and let's say goodnight.'

He released the platter and stepped back, nodding mockingly as he said, 'Goodnight, Elizabeth.'

Then he strode away, back towards the beach, not giving her the chance to say another word.

She was so wound up it took several seconds for her to realise the threat of him was gone—not that he'd been threatening her. It was just how she felt with him, as though in constant danger of having her *rules* undermined or blown apart.

She quickly took the platter to the office desk, set it down and returned to lock the door, telling herself she was now safe for the night. Tomorrow...well, she would deal with tomorrow when it came.

She carried the untouched cake into the apartment, shutting herself into her own private domain. In a violent reaction to the whole stressful day, she found a knife and cut the *Happy Birthday* writing off the icing. It had been a rotten birthday. No happiness at all. She'd suffered a devastating let-down from Michael, as well as what felt like a betrayal from Lucy and persecution from Harry.

Tomorrow had to be better.

She only had to put up with Harry tomorrow.

And while that might not be a piece of cake, she would stomach it somehow.

No way was she going to break up again anywhere near Harry Finn!

CHAPTER NINE

HARRY clenched his hands into fists as he strode back down to the lower deck. The urge to fight was still coursing through him. He'd barely reined it in to bid Elizabeth a fairly civilised goodnight. He certainly didn't *feel* civilised.

Okay, he'd jumped the gun with her but she'd been right there with him. Not one other woman he'd been with had ever pulled back when both of them were fired up to have sex. Being rejected like that was an absolute first, though he probably should have been prepared for it. Elizabeth Flippence had made an art form of rejecting him over the past two years.

What were her damned rules? No mixing business with pleasure? She would have mixed it with Mickey so that didn't wash. Did she have to have a wedding ring on her finger before she'd have sex? Where was she coming from to have that kind of attitude in this day and age? A thirty-year-old virgin? Harry didn't believe it. Not with her looks.

Clearly he needed to know more about her, form another plan of attack because she was *not* going to get away from him. He didn't understand why she dug so deeply under his skin, what made her so compellingly desirable, but the buzz was there and he couldn't get rid of it. What caused him even more frustration was *knowing* she felt the same buzz around him.

It was a maddening situation.

He lifted the bottle of champagne out of the ice bucket, stepped over to the edge of the deck and poured the remaining contents onto the sand. The only thing worse than flat champagne was the flat aftermath of flattened desire. He popped the emptied bottle back in the bucket and started the long walk down the beach to the wharf where his yacht was docked.

He thought of his own birthday—thirty-three last month. Mickey had thrown him a party. They always did that for each other because their parents had and neither of them could quite let go of that golden past, though they had sold the marvellous family property on the hill overlooking Cairns because it wasn't the same—couldn't be—without their mother and father there.

He remembered the great tennis parties and pool parties his mother had organised. His and Mickey's school friends had loved coming to their place—always so much fun to be had. The fishing trips with his father had been great, too. He'd had the best childhood, best teen years, a really happy life until that black day when his father's plane went down.

This resort had still been on the drawing board then. His father had been excited about building it, showing him and Mickey the plans, talking about how he would market it. After the funeral Harry had wanted this project, wanted to be physically busy, creating something, bringing his father's vision to reality. He'd lived here, worked here until it was done, organising everything for it to be a successful enterprise.

Mickey had thrown himself into managing the franchises, needing to be busy, too, both of them wanting to feel their parents would be proud of them. It had seemed the best way to handle their grief, filling the huge hole of loss with hard absorbing work. Neither of them had been interested in managing girlfriends during that dark period, not wanting any emotional demands on them from people who had no understanding of what was driving them. The occasional night out, some casual sex...that had been enough.

Over the years neither he nor Mickey had fallen into any deep and meaningful relationships. Somehow there was always something missing, something that didn't gel, something that put them off. Occasionally they chatted about their various failures to really connect with one woman or another. It always came back to how happy their parents had been together, complementing each other, and ultimately that was what they wanted in a life partner. In the meantime they floated, docking for a while with whatever woman they felt attracted to.

Harry wondered if Lucy would last with Mickey, then chewed over his own problem of even getting a start with Elizabeth.

Why was giving in to a perfectly natural attraction such a problem to her? Why not pursue it, find out if it could lead to a really satisfying relationship? Was she so hung up on her unrequited love for Mickey that she didn't want to admit that something else could be better?

Whatever…he'd get to the bottom of her resistance and smash it, one way or another.

By the next morning Harry had cooled down enough to realise he should give Elizabeth more time to come to terms with the changes in her life. He had rushed her last night. Today he would be very *civilised*. Though not necessarily according to *her* rules.

He had breakfast on the yacht, suspecting that Elizabeth would avoid having breakfast with him in the restaurant. Undoubtedly Miss Efficiency had set her bedside alarm clock for an early hour to be up and about before any of the guests, opening the office and at her desk, ready to deal with anything that came her way. She would certainly have used the convenience of a call to the restaurant to have her breakfast delivered.

As expected, she was at her desk when Harry strolled into the administration office. He beamed a warmly approving smile at her and put a bright lilt in his voice. 'Good morning, Elizabeth.'

It forced her attention away from the computer. She pasted a tight smile on her face and returned his greeting. Her big brown eyes had no shine. They were guarded, watchful. Harry knew her brick wall was up and there would be no easy door through it. The urge to at least put a chink in her defensive armour was irresistible.

He hitched himself onto the corner of the desk, viewing her with curious interest. 'Are you a virgin, Elizabeth?'

That livened up her face, her eyes widening in incredulity and shooting sparks of outrage as she completely lost control of her voice, shrilling, 'What?' at him.

'It's a simple question,' Harry said reasonably. 'Are you a virgin, yes or no?'

'You have no right to ask me that!' she spluttered.

He shrugged. 'Why is it a problem?'

Anger shot to the surface. 'It's none of your business!'

'I guess the answer is yes since you're so sensitive about it,' he tossed at her affably.

'I am *not* sensitive about it!'

'Looks that way to me.'

She glared at him, and if her eyes had been knives they would have stabbed him in a million painful places. Harry found it wonderfully exhilarating. He'd definitely got under her skin again, regardless of how firmly she had decided to keep him out.

Her jaw tightened and he knew she was gritting her teeth as she struggled to bring herself under control. Finally she gnashed out the words 'It's just none of your business, Harry. It is totally irrelevant to this job and I'll thank you to remember that.'

'Bravo!' he said admiringly.

It confused her. 'Bravo what?'

He grinned at her. 'The rule book rules. Almost forgot it there for a moment, didn't you?'

She huffed to release some of the tension he'd raised, viewing him balefully. 'I'd appreciate it if *you* didn't forget it.'

'I do apologise for the transgression.' He made a wry grimace. 'Curiosity slipped through my usual sense of discretion. However, it does give me a better understanding of you now that I know you're a virgin. Head stuffed with romantic dreams...'

'I am *not* a virgin!' tripped out of her mouth before she could stop the wave of exasperation he'd whipped up.

He arched his eyebrows in surprise. 'You're not?'

She closed her eyes. Her mouth shut into

a tight thin line. Quite clearly she hated herself for biting at his bait. Harry revelled in her discomfort. Serve her right for the discomfort she'd given him last night. And it was great to have that problem box ticked off. No virginity barrier.

Another big huff. Her eyes opened into hard, piercing slits. Shards of ice came off her tongue. 'Can we please get down to work now?'

'Jumping to it,' he said obligingly, hitching himself off the desk and rounding it to view the computer screen. 'Any bookings come in this morning?'

'Yes.' She swung her chair around to face the computer and started working the mouse. 'I think I've dealt with them correctly. If you'll check what I've done…?'

For the next half hour Harry kept strictly to business, giving Elizabeth no reason to complain about his behaviour. She had a good understanding of what was required of administration. Supply issues still had to be addressed but that could wait until later. She was so uptight he decided to give her a break, let her relax for a while.

'Before the heat of the day sets in, I'm going to call Jack Pickard to take you around the resort, show you the practical aspects of how it runs. You need to be familiar with all of it,' he said, reaching for the telephone. 'I'll stand in for you here.'

'Okay,' she answered levelly, but the relief he sensed coming from her told him exactly what she was thinking.

Escape.

Escape from the pressure of having to keep denying what was undeniable…the constant sizzle of sexual chemistry between them.

Harry told himself he could wait.

Sooner or later it would come to a head and boil over.

Then he would have her.

Elizabeth took an instant liking to Jack Pickard. She probably would have liked anyone who took her away from Harry this morning but Sarah's husband was a chirpy kind of guy, nattering cheerfully about the island and his maintenance job—easy, relaxing company. He was short and wiry and his weather-beaten face had deep crow's-feet at the corners of his eyes from smiling a lot. His hair looked wiry, too, a mass of unruly curls going an iron-grey.

'Show you one of the vacant villas first.'

He grinned at her. 'Before the new guests fly in this morning.'

'Do they all come by helicopter?' Elizabeth asked.

'Uh-uh. Most come by motor launch. We meet them at the jetty and drive them around to administration. Those that fly in land on the back beach and take the wooden walkway that leads here.'

Wooden walkways led everywhere, with flights of steps wherever they were needed. The one they took to the vacant villa ran through rainforest, the lovely green canopy of foliage above it shading them from the direct heat of the sun. On either side of them were masses of tropical vegetation—palms, vines, bamboo, hibiscus, native flowers.

The villa was situated on a hillside overlooking the bay leading into the main beach. Its front porch had a lovely view and the breeze wafting in from the sea made it a very inviting place to sit in the deckchairs provided. Jack opened a sliding glass door and gestured for her to step inside.

The structure was split-level. Elizabeth entered a spacious living room—a comfortable lounge setting with coffee table facing a television set and CD player, a writing desk and chair, a counter along one wall containing a sink and a bar fridge. Above the counter were cupboards containing a selection of glasses for every kind of drink, bottles of spirits, plus tea and coffee-making facilities, a jar of home-made cookies and a selection of crackers to go with the cheese platter in the fridge, which also held a box of Belgian chocolates, fruit juice, beer, champagne, wine and plenty of drink mixers.

Up a few steps from the living area was a mezzanine bedroom containing a huge king-size bed, lots of pillows, plenty of cupboard space, bedside tables with lamps in the shape of dolphins. All the decor had a sea-and-beach theme, most of the furnishings in white and turquoise, knick-knacky things constructed from driftwood and coral and shells. White walls and polished floorboards completed the clean, airy look.

'There's an extensive library of books, CDs and games in the bar-lounge adjacent to the restaurant,' Jack told her. 'Guests can help themselves to whatever they like. You, too, Elizabeth.'

She smiled at him. 'That's good to know.'

Should fill in some lonely hours, she thought, once Harry was gone and she could

get him out of her mind. That *virgin* question still had her seething, as though *that* was
the only possible reason for not getting her
pants off for him. In hindsight, she probably
should have said she was, put him right off
his game. On the other hand, he might have
fancied himself as teacher, giving her a first
experience in sex. It was impossible to pin
down anything with Harry. He could slide
this way or that way at the blink of an eye.
Which made him so infuriating and frustrating and...

Elizabeth clamped down on those feelings,
forcing herself to focus on what she was seeing here. The bathroom was positively deca-
dent, a shower for two, a spa bath, the walls
tiled in a wavy white with turquoise feature
tiles and turquoise towels. The long vanity
bench held two wash basins and a pretty col-
lection of shells. Everything in the villa was
clearly designed to give guests pleasure.

'This is all fantastic,' she commented to
Jack.

He nodded agreement. 'Sarah and I reckon
Harry did a great job of it.'

'Harry? Surely he had an interior decora-
tor fitting out the villas.'

'Oh, he had a professional finding the stuff

he wanted, but how the villas are all decked out was his idea. His dad had an architect design how they're built. It was his vision in the first place, but after he died, Harry took on the whole project and saw it through to completion. Did a great job of marketing it, too.'

This information did not fit her view of Harry Finn as a playboy. It was disconcerting until she remembered that admirable work and talent had no relevance to how he dealt with women.

She and Jack moved on. He showed her the gym, which contained most of the popular work-out equipment, introducing her to staff she hadn't met yet. A large shed near the beach where the helicopter landed contained a desalination plant that ultimately provided fresh water for the resort. The power generator was also housed there.

'This beach faces west,' Jack said, pointing to the hill above it. 'Up there are the two pavilion villas, both of them occupied today so I can't show them to you. Their porches lead out to infinity pools that catch the sunset. Feels like there's just you and the water and the sky. They weren't on the original plan. Harry's idea to build them, make them really special.'

Elizabeth nodded. 'I noticed it cost more to stay in them.'

Jack grinned. 'Honeymoon paradise.'

As they continued the tour, chatting as they went along, Elizabeth realised her escort was extremely well skilled—electrician, plumber, carpenter, gardener—capable of turning his hand to any maintenance work.

She couldn't help remarking, 'How come you never started a business of your own, Jack? You're so well qualified.'

He grinned. 'Hated all the paperwork the government expects you to do. Reckon I got a plum job with Harry's dad, maintaining the property he had overlooking Cairns. Free cottage, good pay, all the fun of creating and being in a beautiful environment. Got the same deal here on the island with Harry. We've got a good life, Sarah and me. Can't think of anything better.'

'Then you're very lucky,' she said warmly.

'That we are.'

A contented man, Elizabeth thought, wondering if she would ever reach the same state of contentment. Not today. And not here with Harry waiting for her back at the office. It was awful to think of how tempted she had been last night to just let herself be swept up in physical sensation. It had been a long time—almost three years since her last semiserious relationship ended—but that was no reason to engage in casual sex.

She'd never been into bed-hopping. Trying guys out on a purely physical basis did not appeal to her. She needed to feel really connected to the person before taking the next step to absolute intimacy. If Harry considered that attitude a headful of romantic dreams it was because it didn't suit his playboy mentality. Bending her principles for him was not on, though she had to admit he was the sexiest man she had ever met, which made everything wretchedly difficult when she was alone with him.

Just one hour in the office this morning had been exhausting, having to use so much energy blocking out his physical impact on her. Of course, last night's wild interlude had made her even more sexually aware of him. She'd been out of her mind to let him go so far with her. Now she had to cope with that memory in his eyes as well as the memories he'd stamped on her consciousness.

On the walk back to administration, Jack started talking about Harry again, how good he had been at all sports in his teens—that was easy to imagine—and what a pity it was that the untimely death of his parents had caused him to drop them. 'Could have been a champion on any playing field,' was Jack's opinion.

Elizabeth could think of one sport Harry hadn't given up.

He was a champion flirt.

She hoped he wouldn't exercise that particular skill while she had to be with him for the rest of the day. So long as he kept to business, she should be reasonably okay. Nevertheless, it was impossible to stop her nerves twitching in agitation when Jack left her at the office door and Harry swung his chair around from the computer and smiled at her.

'Enjoy the tour?'

She smiled back, deciding to show appreciation of all he'd done here. 'You have created quite an extraordinary resort, Harry. I can't think of anything that could make it better.'

'If you do, let me know. I aim for perfection.'

Would he be the perfect lover?

Elizabeth was shocked at how that thought had slid right past her guard against *the playboy*. She hurled it out of her mind as she hitched herself onto the corner of the desk just as he had this morning, casually asking, 'Anything come in that I should know about?'

'Mickey called. He's putting the suitcase your sister packed for you on the helicopter bringing the guests today.' He gave her a quirky smile. 'Should save you from having to wash out your undies tonight.'

'That's good,' she said equably, determined not to be baited into being prickly.

'Lucy says if she's missed anything you need, send her an email,' Harry went on. 'She'll bring it with her when she comes here with Mickey this weekend.'

Elizabeth sat in frozen suspension.

Her heart stopped.

Her lungs seized up.

Her mind stayed plugged on one horribly chilling thought.

Lucy...coming with Michael...to her island escape from them.

No escape at all!

CHAPTER TEN

HARRY saw her eyes glaze. She sat completely still. He knew this was a crunch moment. He waited, silently speculating on how she would react to the bombshell when she snapped out of the shock wave.

Would pride dictate that she welcome Mickey and her sister onto the island, keeping up the pretence that seeing them together did not hurt her?

Mickey was totally unaware that Elizabeth was hung up on him. So was Lucy. Neither of them would be looking for signs of hurt. It was quite possible to get through this visit, leaving them none the wiser, especially if Elizabeth was willing to let him be the man *she* was interested in. Which had to bring them several steps closer, Harry thought, willing her to choose that path.

Alternatively, since her escape from

Mickey and Lucy had just been scuttled, the island no longer represented a safe refuge for her. And Harry knew he'd gone too far too fast last night, which was certainly ruffling her feathers. She might throw in this job, walk down to the back beach, wait for the helicopter to come in and fly out on it, take a trip somewhere else, not caring what anyone thought—wipe her hands of all of them.

Except she couldn't quite.

Lucy was her sister.

Lucy depended on her to be her anchor and Elizabeth took responsibility seriously. She wasn't the type to cut free. Not completely. But she might want to for a while.

Harry needed to stop her from walking out on him. Having her here on the island was his best chance with her. It gave him time to keep challenging her, wear down her resistance, make her realise they could have something good together.

Elizabeth felt totally numb. It had been such a struggle, holding herself together in front of Michael and Lucy yesterday, a struggle coping with what Harry made her feel, a struggle learning how to manage this resort as fast as she could. Now the whole reason for so much effort, the whole reason for being here was slipping away from her.

She couldn't bear to play out yesterday's scenario with Michael and Lucy again this weekend. It was too much pretence, too much pressure, too much everything with Harry hanging around, ready to take advantage of any weak moment, and she'd be tempted to use him again as a buffer. It was all horribly wrong and the worst part was she was trapped here—trapped by her own deceit.

If she walked out on the job after pretending to like being with Harry, how could she ever explain that to Lucy? It wouldn't make sense. Telling her the truth wasn't fair. It would cut into whatever happiness she was finding with Michael, tarnish it because it was causing her sister unhappiness, which Elizabeth knew Lucy would never knowingly do. Underneath all her ditziness was a very caring heart.

Having taken a deep breath and slowly released it to get her lungs working again and feed some much-needed oxygen into the hopeless morass in her brain, she squared her shoulders and looked directly at Harry Finn—her rescuer and tormentor. There was no devilish twinkle in the blue eyes. They were observing her with sharp attention, alert to any give-away signs of what she was thinking and feeling.

He had demonstrated yesterday how perceptive he was, and remembering how accurately he had read the situation, Elizabeth felt a strong stab of resentment that he hadn't acted to protect her this time.

'You could have dissuaded your brother from coming, Harry,' she said accusingly.

'How?' he challenged. 'By saying you don't want him here? Mickey wants to see if you're managing okay. Both of them do.' His mouth lifted in an ironic tilt. 'I did spring the job on you, Elizabeth.'

'You could have said all the villas were taken—no ready accommodation for them,' she argued.

He shrugged. 'I'm not in the habit of telling lies. Besides, Mickey has a motor-cruiser. They'll be arriving in it and could just as easily sleep in it. A head count of guests at dinner would have told him we have two villas vacant this weekend and he might have confronted me about it, raising questions. Would you have liked to answer them?'

She grimaced, accepting there was no way out of this and there was no point in protesting the arrangements already made. 'Which villa did you put them in?' she asked flatly.

'Mickey requested a pavilion villa if available. Since one of them is vacant from Friday afternoon to Sunday afternoon, I've obliged him.'

A pavilion villa…honeymoon paradise!

She turned her head away, evading Harry's watchful gaze. Flashing through her mind were images of Michael and Lucy enjoying an intimate weekend—making love on the king-size bed, cooling off in the infinity pool, drinking champagne as they watched the sunset. It was sickening. She couldn't help thinking, *It should have been me with Michael. Me, not Lucy.*

For two years she had been dreaming of having just such a romantic weekend with him. Why couldn't he have found her as wildly attractive as he obviously found Lucy? Harry had no problem in seeing her as sexy. He would have whizzed her off to bed in no time flat. Almost had last night.

'They're not coming in until Saturday morning,' Harry said quietly. 'It will only be for one night, Elizabeth.'

As though that made it better, she thought savagely. Lucy would be parading her happiness with Michael from the moment she landed to the moment she waved goodbye, and during that two-day span it was going to be one hell of an uphill battle to keep pretending happiness with Harry.

Unless…

A wicked idea slid into her mind.

It grew, sprouting a whole range of seductive thoughts, becoming a plan that promised a way to get through this weekend reasonably intact.

Harry would view it as a night of fun and games, the playboy triumphant. He wouldn't care about what she was using him for since he'd get what he wanted. And *she* wouldn't be hurt by it because she was the one directing the play, the one in control of what was to happen.

She could set aside her principles, be a butterfly flying free for one night. Maybe it was what she needed to do, use it as a catharsis, releasing all the emotional mess in her mind and heart and wallowing in purely physical sensation. Harry had proved last night he could drive up her excitement meter. Why not experience how far he could take it?

If it was good…if it was great…she could face Lucy and Michael without the horribly hollow sense of missing out on everything, especially since she would have already had what they were going to have and where they were going to have it. That part of it should kill off any sense of jealousy and envy, which were horribly negative feelings that she didn't want to have towards her sister. Lucy was Lucy. It wasn't her fault that Michael was totally smitten by her, and Elizabeth was not going to let *their* connection affect the close relationship she'd always had with her sister.

But she needed help from Harry to make all this stick.

His expert playboy help, smashing her mind with so much pleasure it took away the pain.

If he didn't cooperate with her plan… But he would, wouldn't he? He wanted her to *surrender* herself to him and that was what she'd be doing.

She threw a quick glance at him. He was leaning back in the chair, apparently relaxed as he waited for her to respond to the situation. However, his gaze instantly caught hers, sharply searching for what was in her mind. There was no point in taking any evasive action. She had decided on what she wanted

from him. Her own eyes watched his very
keenly as she put the question which would
start a new situation rolling.

'Do you still want to have sex with me,
Harry?'

His eyebrows shot up in surprise. There
was no instant *yes.* Elizabeth's heart pounded
nervously as she waited for his reply, watching his eyes narrow speculatively. He was
obviously digesting what this change from
her meant.

'That's been a constant for me over quite a
long time, Elizabeth,' he said slowly. 'I think
the more pertinent question is do you finally
realise that you want to have sex with me?'

'Yes, I do,' she answered unequivocally.
'But only if certain conditions are met.'

It had to be her plan or nothing.

His head tilted to one side. He was not
rushing to accommodate her. His eyes
watched her with an even higher level of
intensity. Elizabeth held his gaze defiantly,
determined not to budge from this stance.
After a long nerve-racking silence, he casually waved a hand in an invitational gesture.

'Spell out the conditions.'

Elizabeth took a deep breath, fiercely
willing him to fall in with what she wanted.

'The pavilion villa is empty on Friday night.
I want it to be there. And then. The rest of
this week we just keep to business.'

It took every ounce of Harry's control not
to react violently, to absorb this slug to his
guts and remain seated, appearing to be con-
sidering what all his instincts were savagely
railing against. This wasn't about him and
the chemistry between them. It was about
Mickey and Lucy. In some dark twisted place
in her mind, she probably wanted to pretend
he was his brother, having it off in the same
romantic setting where Mickey was about to
take her sister.

No way would he be used as a freaking
substitute!

It was a bitter blow to his ego that she
should ask it of him. It showed how little she
cared about what he thought, what he felt. He
had encouraged her to use him as a blind to
hide her angst over Mickey yesterday but to
use him this far…it was brutal and he hated
her for corrupting what they could have had
together.

Hate…

He'd never felt that towards anyone. Why
did she get to him so strongly? It was crazy.

He should wipe her off his slate right now, find some other woman who thought he was worth having, who'd be sweetly giving, at least for a while.

Except…damn it! He still wanted the ungettable Elizabeth Flippence!

Have her and be done with it, he thought savagely.

He could use her scenario his way, add his own conditions, make her so hyped up with sexual awareness, Mickey would be blotted right out of her mind and he'd be *the man*—the only man she'd be conscious of all through the night.

She was patiently waiting for his agreement, her eyes boring into his, boldly challenging his desire for her. He sensed that some essential part of her had clicked off. She'd moved beyond caring what he said or did. The equation was simple. He either went with her plan or that was the end of anything personal ever happening between them.

'Okay,' he said calmly. 'I'll make arrangements for us to occupy the pavilion villa on Friday night.'

She nodded, the expression in her eyes changing to a knowing mockery. She had labelled him a playboy on quite a few occa-

sions so he knew what she was thinking—
a night of sex would always be amenable to
him, regardless of why it was offered.

He decided to live up to her idea of him.

'As long as you'll fit in with some conditions I have in mind,' he said with a quirky
little smile.

That shot some tension through her. 'Like
what?' she asked sharply.

'Like not saying no to anything I want to
do.'

She frowned. 'I won't do kinky stuff, Harry.'

'I'm not into sado-masochism, domination
or bondage,' he assured her. 'But I don't particularly care for clinical intimacy, either. A
bit of sexy fun is more to my liking.'

'What do you consider sexy fun?' she
asked suspiciously.

He grinned. 'How about you wear that
butterfly blouse again, without a bra underneath? Be *wicked* for me.'

Hot colour raced up her neck and scorched
her cheeks. Harry didn't care if she connected the butterfly blouse to her Mickey
fantasy. He'd had a few fantasies about it
himself.

'And team it with a bikini bottom with
side strings that I can undo with a flick of

the fingers,' he added. 'Some bright colour that goes with your butterfly. I'm sure you'll be able to find one in the boutique.'

She rolled her eyes. 'I didn't realise you needed provocative clothes to turn you on, Harry.'

He shrugged. 'I don't. I'd simply like you to look and be accessible for once. I've been hitting a brick wall with you for two years. *Accessible* has a lot of appeal to me.'

Her cheeks heated up again, making her eyes look glittery. 'Do you have anything else in mind?' she clipped out.

He waved an airy hand. 'Let me think about it. You have rather sprung this on me. If I'm only to ever get one night with Elizabeth Flippence...' He cocked an eyebrow at her. 'That is the plan, isn't it?'

'Yes' hissed out between her teeth.

'Then I want it to be a night to remember. Something extra special. The most sensual trip of a lifetime. I need to let my imagination work on it for a while.'

'Fine!' she snapped, and hopped off the desk, adopting a brisk and businesslike air. 'You have three and a half days for your imagination to flourish. Since we have the essentials settled, let's get on with resort management.'

He could almost hear the steel click in her mind. In his experience of women, Elizabeth Flippence was definitely something else. But she would soften for him on Friday night. He'd make damned sure she did!

He rose from the chair. 'I've brought up the file on all our suppliers on the computer. Go through it. Write down any questions you have and I'll be back later to answer them. Okay?'

'Okay.'

Her relief that he was leaving her to work alone was palpable.

He strode quickly out of the office, needing time apart from her, too. He was still churned up inside. A work-out in the gym should rid him of the violent energy that was currently coursing through him.

Three and a half days…

He wondered if he'd feel free of this mad obsession with Elizabeth Flippence after Friday night. He really was beginning to hate how much she got to him. Probably she hated how he got to her, too.

Was having sex the answer to settling everything?

Impossible to know beforehand.

Afterwards…

That should tell him whether to persist with trying to form a relationship with this infuriating woman or let her go. It all hung on one night and—by God!—he was going to make the most of it!

CHAPTER ELEVEN

ELIZABETH found herself rebelling against any regret over her decision to take Harry Finn as her lover for one night. It might be stupidly reckless of her to have sex with him. There would probably be consequences she wouldn't like but she refused to care about what could happen next. Just for once she would be totally irresponsible, except for the important issue of birth control, which was impossible to ignore.

She tackled Harry on that point as soon as he returned to the office. 'I'm not on the pill,' she stated bluntly. 'Will you take care of contraception on Friday night?'

'No problem,' he blithely replied. 'And incidentally, I've thought of another condition.'

Elizabeth tensed. If it was too outlandish…

'When we're in the villa, I want to call you Ellie.'

She was startled into asking, 'Why?'

He shrugged. 'A childhood name, conjuring up the age of innocence. I like that idea.'

'I'm not innocent, Harry.' Surely he couldn't still be thinking she was a virgin.

'Nevertheless, it's what I want. Okay?'

She shook her head over his whimsy but… what did it matter? 'If it pleases you,' she said carelessly.

'It *will* please me,' he asserted, then smiled at her. 'I also want to please you. If you think of anything you'd particularly enjoy on the night, let me know. Your wish is my command.'

'I prefer to leave everything in your very capable hands, Harry,' she said dryly, not wanting to think too much about it.

But she did over the next couple of days. And nights. It was weird how completely distracted she was from thinking about Michael and Lucy. The now-certain prospect of having sex with Harry made her more physically aware of him than ever, and the anticipation of it was zinging through her almost continually.

He didn't come up with any more conditions, didn't raise the subject at all, keeping their time together on a strictly business basis, as she had requested. Somehow that contributed to a sense of secretive intimacy, knowing what they were going to do when Friday night came but not mentioning it.

She found a red string bikini in the boutique and bought it, deciding it suited the occasion since she was acting like a scarlet woman, taking a lover she didn't love. Oddly enough she felt no guilt about doing it. Somehow it represented the kind of freedom she probably wouldn't feel with someone she did love. There were no dreams to be smashed, no expectations of sharing a life together. It was just a night of sexy fun with Harry Finn.

On Friday morning, Harry announced he had business in Port Douglas and would be gone for most of the day. He printed a notice that the office would be closed at 6:00 p.m. today and stuck it on the door. 'Go on up to the villa then,' he instructed. 'I'll be there. Don't want to miss the sunset,' he added with a smile that sparkled with anticipation.

'I'll bring a bottle of champagne from the bar,' she said, remembering how she had envisaged the scene with Michael and Lucy.

'No need. I'll have one ready to open.'

'What about food? Shall I order…?'

He shook his head. 'I have that organised, as well. You only have to bring yourself, Elizabeth.' He raised his hand in a farewell salute. 'Bye for now. Have a nice day.'

'You, too,' she replied, smiling back at him.

It was a genuine smile, not the slightest bit forced. Not having to keep her guard up against him all the time had made her more relaxed in his company. She had nothing to guard against since she was giving in to what he wanted from her. And if she was completely honest with herself, she wanted it, too.

He was a sexy man.

He made her feel sexy.

She was looking forward to having this experience with Harry tonight. She probably would have hated herself if she'd been seduced into it, but the sense of empowerment that came with having decided on it herself made all the difference.

Nevertheless, when six o'clock came and she was on her way to the pavilion villa, her nerves started getting very jumpy. She had never had an assignation like this before. It was totally out of character for her. But there was no turning back from it, she told herself fiercely. Everything was in place to take this step, and take it she would.

Harry was standing by the infinity pool, looking out to sea. He wore only a pair of board shorts, printed with white sailing ships on a blue background. She paused on the last step leading to the open deck, her heart skittering at the sight of so much naked masculinity—broad shoulders tapering to lean hips, bronze skin gleaming over taut, well-defined muscles. He had the perfect male physique and it tugged on some deeply primitive female chord in Elizabeth.

It was okay to feel attracted to him, she told herself.

It was natural.

On the physical level.

As though sensing her presence he swung around, his gaze instantly targeting her, piercing blue eyes raking her from head to toe, making her hotly conscious that she was still in the island uniform. She quickly held up the carry bag holding the clothes he'd requested and gabbled an explanation.

'I've just finished at the office, Harry. I thought I'd take a shower here.'

He nodded. 'Make it fast. The sun is already low in the sky.'

The glass doors to the villa were open. The layout inside was similar to the one Jack had shown her. She headed straight for the bathroom, anxious not to be found wanting in keeping to her side of their deal. One minute to turn on the shower taps and strip off her clothes, two minutes under the refreshing beat of the water, one minute to towel herself dry, one minute to pull on the red bikini bottom and put on the butterfly blouse, fastening only one button to keep it more or less together.

Accessible was what he'd asked for. He couldn't say she wasn't delivering it. The shape of her braless breasts and the darker colour of her areolae were certainly visible through the sheer fabric, and her nipples were already stiffening, poking at the butterfly wings. She hoped he had the champagne ready. Carrying this much accessibility off with any air of confidence required some alcoholic fortification.

It was only on her exit from the bathroom that Elizabeth caught a waft of nose-teasing scent coming from the mezzanine level. She looked up to where the king-size bed was waiting for intimate activity. Candles—from small to large—lit a path to it. A long sniff identified their fragrance as frangipani, the flower most reminiscent of tropical nights.

Harry must have set them up. Had he bought them in Port Douglas today? Why go to the trouble? This was not a night of romance. Did he want her to imagine it was? And why should he want that? She didn't understand. But it was…nice of him to do it.

She was smiling over what she had decided was playboy fun as she walked out onto the deck. 'Do you treat all your women to scented candles?' she asked.

He was about to pop the cork of a bottle of champagne. He paused to give her a very long, all-encompassing look that made her extremely conscious of every female part of her body. 'No. I simply associate the scent of flowers with butterflies, Ellie. An innocent pleasure,' he said softly.

His use of her childhood name instantly reminded her of how he'd linked it to an age of innocence. She wished she knew what was going on in his mind. It seemed to be off on some quirky journey tonight.

He popped the cork and reached for one of the flute glasses sitting on the low table that served the sun-lounges. A plate of lush fresh strawberries was placed beside the ice bucket that awaited the opened bottle. As he poured the champagne, Elizabeth saw that a couple of crushed strawberries lay in the bottom of the glass, making it a very sensual drink.

'Enjoy,' he said as he passed it to her, his smile inviting her to share all sorts of pleasure with him.

'Thank you, Harry,' she said appreciatively, grateful that he wasn't grabbing at her *accessibility* or doing anything off-putting.

He waved her to one of the sun-lounges. 'Relax. Looks like being a spectacular sunset.'

She sat on the lounge, not quite ready to put herself on display by stretching out on it. Harry poured champagne for himself, then clicked her glass with his. 'To our first night together,' he said, smiling as he dropped onto the adjacent lounge, propped himself against the backrest, lifted his long legs onto the cushioned base and gazed out to a sea that was shimmering like polished crystal.

It released Elizabeth's inhibitions about doing the same. This villa certainly had a prime position for viewing the sunset. The subtle colour changes in the sky would challenge any artist—impossible to capture on canvas, she thought. It truly was lovely, just watching it and sipping strawberry-flavoured champagne.

'Have you ever been to Broome?' Harry asked.

'No.' Broome was right across the country on the coast of Western Australia. She knew it was world famous for its pearls but she'd never had any reason to go there. 'Why do you ask?'

'Sunset there is amazing. People drive down on the beach, set up their barbecues, bring eskies loaded with cold drinks, play music, sit back and enjoy Mother Nature's display for them. They completely tune out from news of the world and just live in the moment.'

He rolled the words out in a low, almost spellbinding tone that was soothing, like a physical caress that eased the last threads of tension in Elizabeth's body.

'We don't do enough of it...living in the moment,' he went on in the same seductive murmur. 'Let's try to do that tonight, Ellie. No yesterdays...no tomorrows...just each moment as it comes.'

'Yes,' she agreed, happy with the idea.

They sipped their champagne in silence

for a while, watching the sun slowly disappear below the horizon.

'My parents used to do this…have a sundowner together at the end of the day,' Harry said, slanting her a reminiscent little smile. 'What about yours, Ellie? Do they have a special time to themselves?'

She shook her head. 'My mother died of cancer when I was nineteen. I haven't seen my father since the funeral. He's a miner and living with some other woman in Mt Isa. It was never much of a marriage. Mum more or less brought Lucy and me up by herself.'

Harry frowned at her. 'Your father doesn't care about you?'

She grimaced. 'I think we were responsibilities he didn't really want. Mostly when he came home on leave from the mine, he'd get drunk and we'd stay out of his way.'

'What about when your mother became ill?'

'He came home less. Didn't want to be faced with what was happening to Mum. He said it was up to me and Lucy to take care of her.'

'That must have been hard,' Harry said sympathetically.

'Yes. Though it was a special time, too.

Like you said…living in the moment…because the last moment could come at any time so every good moment was precious.'

'At least you knew that,' he murmured, nodding understandingly before throwing her a wry little smile. 'Mickey and I… we didn't realise how precious those good moments were until after our parents were gone.'

'I guess that kind of sudden death is harder to come to terms with,' she said thoughtfully.

'I don't know. We didn't have to see them suffer.' He shook his head. 'You were only nineteen. How did you manage?'

'I was at business college so I could be home quite a lot. Lucy dropped out of school to look after Mum when I couldn't be there.'

'Did she pick up her education again at a later date?'

'No.' Impossible to explain that school had never been easy for Lucy. She didn't like people knowing about her dyslexia. 'She didn't want to, didn't need it to get work.'

'But without qualifications…'

'Lucy is adept at winning her way into jobs.'

'While you're the one with the steady career. That's why she calls you her anchor.'

Elizabeth heaved a sigh. 'This is a weird conversation to be having when we're supposed to be enjoying a night of sexy fun, Harry.'

'Oh, I don't know. I'd call this an intimate conversation. We have all night to get to physical intimacy. We've been on the fringes of each other's worlds for two years. I think I know Elizabeth fairly well—' he rolled his head towards her, giving her his quirky smile '—but I want to get to know Ellie tonight.'

'That's yesterday, Harry. My childhood,' she pointed out. 'It's not living in the moment.'

The blue eyes gathered the piercing intensity that always gave her discomfort. 'Ellie is inside you right now,' he said softly. 'She's the foundation of the woman you are. She directs your life.'

'That's ridiculous!' she protested.

'Is it? You're the older child, the one who helped your mother, the one who protected your sister, the one who carried the responsibility of arranging everything when your mother was ill, when she died, the one who wants a man in her life who will never do to her what her father did to her mother, to his children.'

He was digging at her again—digging, digging, digging! In a burst of frustration, Elizabeth swung her legs off the lounge, sat up straight and glared at him. 'I did not come up here to be psychoanalysed, Harry.'

He swung his legs down to the deck in a more leisurely fashion, his eyes holding hers in glittering challenge. 'No, you didn't. Ellie wanted to break out of the Elizabeth cocoon and fly free for once, didn't she?'

She hated how he could connect everything up and be so damned right about everything! It made her feel naked in far more than the physical sense. In a purely defensive action, she snatched the bottle of champagne from the ice bucket, intending to refill her glass.

Harry took it from her. 'Allow me.'

She did, letting him pour the champagne, though it made her feel he was taking control away from her, which wasn't how she'd planned to have this encounter with Harry. 'Do you probe into the lives of all your one-night stands?' she asked waspishly.

He cocked an eyebrow at her. 'What makes you think my life consists of a series of one-night stands?'

'The way you flirt. Michael said you flirt with every woman. It isn't just me.'

'Flirting can be fun. It can be enjoyable to both parties. In a way it's a search for that magic click which will lead to bed, but that doesn't happen very often. When it has, I can't recall one instance when it only lasted for one night. You've assumed something about me that isn't true, Ellie.'

'Well, this is only going to be for one night,' she insisted, needing to regain the control that seemed to be sliding out of her grip.

'Why?'

'Because...' She floundered, not wanting to say the whole idea had erupted from the fact his brother was going to be here with her sister and she hadn't really looked beyond that painful circumstance. 'I just don't want to get heavily involved with you, Harry,' she said evasively, wishing he would simply accept what she'd offered him.

'Why not? You think I'll let you down?'

Yes was on the tip of her tongue but he didn't give her time to say it.

'Did I let you down when you needed to cover up your distress over Mickey attaching himself to your sister? Did I let you down when you needed an escape from them? Have I let you down in fulfilling your requests this week, meeting what you wanted? Haven't I shown I care about how you feel, Ellie?'

She couldn't deny any of that, yet… 'It…it fitted into your own agenda,' she blurted out.

'Which is?' He bored in.

Her head was spinning from the pressure he was subjecting her to with all his questions. She had to seize on the one point she was certain of, drive it home. She set her glass on the table, stood up, challenging him to get on with what he'd been aiming for all along.

'Having me like this! *Accessible!*' She threw the words at him. 'So why don't you stop talking and take what you want with me?'

Anger burned through Harry. He'd tried to reach out to her, tried to find a special meeting ground with her. She just kept closing her mind, shutting the door on him, keeping him out. He set his glass down, rose to his feet and hurled her confrontation right back in her face.

'You want to be treated like a piece of meat instead of a woman I care about? Fine! Just stand there and let me oblige!'

CHAPTER TWELVE

HARRY saw her eyes dilate with shock.

He didn't care.

She'd invited him to take her without caring and his level of frustration with her was so high, turning away from following through on her invitation was beyond him. His hands lifted and cupped the breasts they'd wanted to cup in Mickey's office days ago. He fanned her rock-hard nipples with his thumbs. The soft sheer fabric of the butterfly blouse gave a sensual sexiness to feeling her like this, causing a rush of hot blood to his loins.

He wanted her.

He'd been burning up for her all week.

Her eyes refocused on his, still slightly glazed but clearing as she sucked in a deep breath.

Yes, look at me! he thought savagely. *Know it's me and not Mickey!*

He undid the button holding her blouse together and spread the edges apart, wanting to feel the naked lushness of her breasts against his chest. His arms slid around her waist, scooping her into firm contact with him. It felt good. It felt great.

'Harry...' It was a husky gasp.

He didn't want to hear anything she had to say. His name on her lips shot a soaring wave of triumph through him—*his* name, not Mickey's—and he was hell-bent on keeping it stamped on her consciousness. His mouth crashed onto hers, intent on a blitzkrieg invasion that would blast any possible thought of his brother from entering her head.

To his surprise her tongue started duelling with his and a wild elation burst through his brain when her hands clutched his head, not to tear them apart but to hold them together, her fingers kneading his scalp, her mouth working to meet and escalate the passion surging through him.

He pressed one hand into the sexy pit of her back, forcing her body into contact with his erection as he pulled the bikini string at her hip apart, changed hands to do the same with the other, whipped the scrap of fabric from between her legs. The lovely female curves of her naked bottom were sensual dynamite, igniting his need for her to the brink of explosion.

He tore his hands off them to sweep the blouse from her shoulders and pull it off her arms. It broke her hold on his head, broke the marauding madness of their kissing, but it had to be done. She was fully naked now, totally *accessible* to anything he wanted with her.

He bent and scooped her off her feet, holding her crushed to his chest as he strode from the deck, into the villa, up the steps to the mezzanine level. He tumbled her onto the king-size bed, snatched up the contraceptive sheath he'd laid ready on the bedside table, discarded his board shorts in double-quick time, pulled on the sheath and leapt onto the bed, rolling her straight into his embrace, not allowing any sense of separation to strike any doubts about what they were doing in her mind.

Their mouths locked again, driving passion to fever pitch. Her body was arching into his, explicitly needful. He barely controlled the urge to zero in to the ultimate intimacy with her. Only the bitter recollection of her *one night* insistence forced him to a different course of action. If this was all there was to be between them he'd satisfy every desire she'd ever stirred in him—eat her all up so he could spit her out afterwards, not be left fantasising over what he could have done.

He wrenched his mouth from hers, trailed hotly possessive kisses down her lovely long neck, tasted the tantalising hollow at the base of her throat, slid lower to feast on her sensational breasts, swirling his tongue around her provocative nipples, sucking on them, devouring them, taking his fill of her luscious femininity, revelling in the little moans vibrating from her throat, the twist of her fingers tangling with his hair.

He reached down to part the soft folds of her sex, his own fingers sliding, searching, finding the excited wetness that gave him easy entry to stroke the excitement to a much-higher level. She cried out, her body arching again, her need growing in intensity. He moved lower, determined on driving her crazy for him.

He spread the folds apart to expose the tight bud of her clitoris and licked it, slowly teasing at first, then faster, faster until she was writhing, screaming for him, begging, her legs encircling him, feet beating a drum of wild wanting. He surged up to take the ultimate plunge, but the savage need inside him demanded a last absolute surrender from her.

Her head was thrashing from side to side. He held it still. 'Look at me!' he commanded.

She blinked and looked but there was no real focus in her eyes.

'Say my name!'

'What?' It was a gasp of confusion.

'Say my name!'

'Har...ry...' It was a weak waver of sound.

'Say it again!'

'Harry, Harry, Harry...' she cried hysterically. 'Please...'

'You want me?'

'Ye-s-s-s.' She beat at his shoulders with tightly clenched fists. 'I'll kill you if you don't...'

He silenced her with a deep, thrusting kiss as he propelled his flesh into hers. When he lifted his head, the animal groan of satisfaction from her throat rang jubilant bells in his ears. She clutched his buttocks, trying to goad him into a fast rhythm, but he wanted the excitement to build and build, not explode all at once. He started slowly, revelling in her eagerness for him, the convulsive little spasms that told him she was totally engaged in feeling him—*him*, not Mickey.

He felt her creaming around him and couldn't keep controlling the rampantly growing need of his own body. It overtook his mind, oblivious to everything but the physical scream to reach climax, releasing the fierce tension raging through every muscle of his body. It pumped from him in a glorious burst of ecstatic satisfaction, and with all tension draining away, he rolled onto his side, pulling her with him, wanting to hang on to the sense of intimate togetherness as long as he could.

She didn't attempt any move away from him. Maybe she was drained of all energy, too. Whatever…she left her legs entwined with his, their bodies pressed close, her head tucked under his chin. He stroked her hair, enjoying the soft silky texture of it, thinking he still had the freedom to touch. He wondered how she was going to act for the rest of the night. Would Ellie emerge and see him for the man he was, or would Elizabeth stick to her guns?

He couldn't call it.

He told himself he didn't care.

At least he had the satisfaction of making her want him with every fibre of her being, if only for one night.

Elizabeth didn't want to move. It felt unbelievably good, cuddled up with Harry, having her hair stroked. Her mind drifted to her childhood, sitting on her mother's lap, head resting just like this while her hair was stroked lovingly. No one else had ever done it. She'd always been the one to comfort Lucy, not the other way around. It was weird, feeling comforted by Harry but...she didn't want to move.

She liked being naked with him, too, the warm flesh contact, the sense of his male strength holding her safe. It was so nice and peaceful after the storm of incredible sensation. Having sex with Harry...her mind was still blown by it...just totally unimaginable before experiencing it. She'd never tipped so utterly out of control, never been taken to such peaks of exquisite pleasure-pain, and the sheer ecstasy of floating in the aftermath of one climax after another...well, that had certainly set the bar for how fantastic sex with the right man could be.

Though she hadn't thought Harry was the

right man in any other respect…or…might
he be?

Maybe she had been a bit too quick to
judge, misreading his character. Or maybe
she was just being influenced by how *right*
he was in bed for her. Most probably he was
the best action man on that front for every
woman he took to bed. Just because this had
been special to her didn't make it special to
him. But she was still glad she'd had this
with Harry.

'Are you okay?' he murmured caringly.

She sighed contentedly. 'Very okay, thank
you.'

'Then let's go take a shower. Once we're
done there we can get in the pool and cool
off.'

She *was* hot and sticky. 'Good idea,' she
said.

The shower was more than big enough for
two and Elizabeth was in no hurry using it
this time. She enjoyed soaping Harry's great
body, touching him intimately, letting him
do the same to her.

'Having fun?'

The wry note in his voice made her look
up. There was no amusement twinkling in
the vivid blue eyes. The mocking glint in

them dried up the pleasure she had been feeling, sending a chill through her as she remembered her taunt about having a night of sexy fun, rejecting having any deeper involvement with him, virtually dismissing him as a person of no account in her life. He'd been so angry—*shockingly* angry. She'd forgotten that, her mind swamped by so much else.

Instinctively she reached up to touch his cheek in an apologetic appeal. 'I was taking pleasure in you, Harry. I thought you were taking pleasure in me.'

For a moment his mouth took on an ironic twist. Then he bent his head and kissed her, a long sensual kiss that swallowed up any worry about him still being angry with her.

Finishing off in the infinity pool was another sensual pleasure, the water like cool silk caressing her skin. 'Just stay there,' Harry instructed as he heaved himself out. 'I'll light the torches to keep the insects away and bring out the oysters with some chilled wine.'

'Oysters!' She laughed. 'I don't think I need an aphrodisiac, Harry.'

He stopped. His shoulders squared and she saw his back muscles tense. He half turned to face her, a cutting look in his eyes that ripped through the amusement in hers. 'I'm not into playboy tricks, Elizabeth. I simply remembered you liked them at your birthday lunch.'

That coldly spoken *Elizabeth* slapped her with the realisation that she was offending him every time she painted him as a playboy. Perhaps even insulting him. He'd told her straight out that the label was wrong in his eyes. Had she been doing him an injustice all this time? What hard evidence did she actually have that he used women lightly? None!

There was a sitting shelf at one end of the pool, and she settled on it, still enjoying the soft ripple of the water around her dangling legs as she thought back over the two years Harry had been dipping into her life while she'd been working for his brother. When he'd first walked into her office he'd emanated a megawatt attraction that had put her in such a tizzy physically she had instantly mistrusted and disliked his power to do that to her.

She'd reasoned that a man with so much personal magnetism was very likely to stray from any relationship since other women would always be eyeing him over, wanting a chance with him, especially when he was both wealthy and sexy. Determined not to go anywhere near that playing field, she had kept a rigid guard against his insidious assaults on her armour.

Now it felt as though she had prejudiced herself against a man who might well be worth knowing in a deeper sense than she had ever believed possible. Could he actually fulfil everything she had been looking for? His brother had definitely been more the type of character that appealed to her—solid, responsible—not dangerous like Harry. Yet Michael had not seen what he wanted in her. And was Harry really dangerous, or was that a false perception on her part?

She watched him emerge from the villa and stroll across the deck towards her, carrying a platter of oysters, a bottle of wine and two fresh glasses. He'd tucked a white towel around his waist. The sky had darkened and the flickering light of the torches he'd lit at the corners of the deck was not bright enough for her to see the expression in his eyes. Was he still angry with her?

'Shall I get out?' she asked.

'Not if you don't want to,' he answered

with a careless shrug. 'I can serve you just as easily there.'

'The water's lovely.'

'Then stay.'

He set the platter on the deck, sat on the edge of the pool and proceeded to open the bottle of wine and fill the glasses.

'I do like oysters, Harry. Thank you for remembering,' she said, hoping to erase the *aphrodisiac* remark.

He handed her the glass of white wine with a droll little smile. 'I remembered your sister saying you loved chilli mud crab, too. I know a restaurant in Port Douglas that specialises in that dish so I had it cooked for you and it's waiting in the microwave to be heated up when you want it.'

She stared at him, horribly shamed by his caring and generosity when she had treated him so meanly, using him as a distraction, even to going to bed with him in this villa because of Michael bringing Lucy here.

'I'm sorry,' she blurted out.

He frowned. 'Sorry about what?'

'My whole attitude towards you. It's been uncaring and bitchy and...and soured by things that you weren't even a part of. I haven't been fair to you, Harry. I've never been fair to you and I don't know why you're being so nice to me because I don't deserve it.' Tears suddenly welled into her eyes and she quickly tried to smear them away with the back of her hand. 'I'm sorry. I'm all messed up and I can't help myself.'

'It's okay,' he said soothingly. 'Just take a few deep breaths and let it all go. Life is a bitch sometimes. The trick is to get past the bad bits. I've been trying to help you do that, Ellie.'

Ellie… The soft caring way her childhood name rolled off his tongue brought another spurt of tears to her eyes and screwed her up inside, stirring up the craven wish for someone to take care of her. She'd been taking care of herself and Lucy for so long, she needed someone to simply be there for her. But she couldn't expect Harry to keep doing that. She didn't know how far his kindness would stretch. What she could do was bask in it for a little while.

It took quite a few deep breaths to bring herself under control enough to manage a smile at him. 'Thank you for helping me.'

'You do deserve to have nice things done for you,' he said seriously. 'Everyone does. It makes the world a happier place. My mother taught me that. She was brilliant at it.'

She sipped the wine he had poured for her, remembering Sarah Pickard's description of Yvette Finn—*a sunny nature, radiating a joy in life that infected everyone around her.* 'Sarah said you're like your mother,' she remarked, starting to reappraise the man in a completely different light to how she had previously perceived him.

He gave a wry shake of his head. 'A hard act to follow, but I try.'

'Tell me about her,' she said impulsively, wanting to understand where Harry was coming from.

He made an indecisive gesture. 'Where to start?'

'Start with how your father met her,' she encouraged.

He laughed. 'In hospital. He'd broken his leg and Mum was the only nurse who wouldn't let him be grumpy.'

'She was an ordinary common nurse?' It surprised her, having imagined that Franklyn Finn would have married some beautiful accomplished socialite.

Harry shook his head. 'I don't think anyone would have said she was ordinary. All the patients loved her, my father included. He always considered himself extremely privileged that she learned to love him back. It took him quite some time to win her.'

'She didn't like him at first?'

'It wasn't that. She wasn't sure about how she would fit into his life. Dad was a seriously driven guy. In the end, she made up a set of rules for how their marriage could work and he had to promise to keep to them.'

'Did he?'

'Never wavered from them. She was the light of his life and he was never going to let that light go out.' He grimaced. 'In a way, I guess it was a kind fate that they died together. They were so tied to each other.'

It must have been a wonderful marriage, Elizabeth thought, wishing she could have one like it. Her own mother hadn't known much happiness in hers and the end of her life had certainly not been kind, though she and Lucy had done their best to ease the pain of it. 'I always thought Lucy could have made a great nurse,' she murmured, remembering how good she had been at cheering up their mother.

'She could have become one if she'd wanted to,' Harry remarked.

'No' slipped out before she could stop it.

'Why not? She could have gone back to school....'

'Lucy was never good at exams,' she prevaricated. Her dyslexia made it impossible for her to pass them. She was smart enough to pick up anything as an apprentice and she had a great memory, but examinations that required reading and writing within a set time simply couldn't be done. 'I don't think she had the head for study after Mum died,' she added to put him off pursuing the point. 'She was only seventeen and she took it hard, Harry.'

'Understandable,' he said sympathetically.

She sipped some more of the wine and eyed the platter of oysters. 'I think I'm ready to eat now.'

He laughed. 'Help yourself.'

'I'll get out first.'

Harry quickly rose to his feet, grabbing a towel to dry her off and wrap around her. She didn't try to take it from him and didn't protest his action when he finished up tucking it around her waist, leaving her breasts bare. 'They're too beautiful to cover up,' he said with a smile.

'I'm glad you think so,' she said a little shyly.

Exhilaration zinged through Harry. She'd dropped all the barriers. There was no rejection in her eyes, no guard up against him. And it remained like that for the rest of the evening, no bitchy barbs slung at him, no hiding what she thought or felt about anything, no shutting him out.

She might not have forgotten all about Mickey but she had definitely put his brother aside and was actively taking pleasure in finding connections with him—connections beyond the purely physical. The sexual chemistry was still there, of course, simmering between them, heightened by their newly intimate knowledge of each other, but Harry was encouraged to believe this could actually be the beginning of a relationship that might become very special.

He wasn't driven to carry her off to bed in a fury of frustration a second time. She happily walked with him and they both indulged in slow, sensual lovemaking—a sweet pleasuring of each other that was intensely satisfying to Harry. No way was this going to be a one-night stand. He wouldn't accept that. Elizabeth Flippence had opened up to

him and he liked it too much to let her slip
away from him.

Tomorrow he would see if her attachment
to Mickey had been broken.

He wanted it broken.

It had to be broken.

CHAPTER THIRTEEN

A WOMAN I care about...

Those words spoken last night kept running through Elizabeth's mind all morning, keeping any anxiety over coming face to face with Michael and Lucy again at bay. She added up all the caring from Harry and realised no other man in her life had done as much for her—helping, comforting, pleasuring, answering her needs.

It couldn't be just about having sex with her.

There had been genuine concern in his eyes when he'd asked, 'Are you going to be okay today?' before leaving her at the office door after their night at the pavilion villa.

She'd assured him that she would be and he'd added, 'I'll be on hand.'

Ready to run interference if she needed it, as he had last Monday.

It felt really good to have him caring about her—someone she could depend on to get her through this weekend without too much heartache. Oddly enough, she wasn't feeling any heartache at all over Michael wanting Lucy, although seeing them together again might strain her current sense of being able to set them at an emotional distance.

Harry was to meet them at the jetty and transport them to the administration centre. Elizabeth felt reasonably confident about handling their queries about how well she was coping with management responsibilities. Lucy, of course, would angle for a private conversation with her, but she didn't think that would trouble her too much. She no longer felt so shattered over her lost dreams.

A few guests dropped into the office to check on arrangements they'd made for diving expeditions. There were inquiries about bookings to be answered. A couple of beach picnics had to be sorted out with the chef. Sarah Pickard came by, ostensibly to put in an order for new towels, but her eyes shone with lively curiosity about this new development between Harry and his stand-in manager.

Probably all the staff on the island knew

about it by now since the villa had to be cleaned this morning, ready for Michael and Lucy. Elizabeth had decided it didn't matter but she certainly wasn't going to talk about her private life to anyone.

'Harry said it's your sister coming with Mickey today,' Sarah remarked.

'Yes,' Elizabeth answered briefly.

'That's nice.'

Elizabeth smiled. 'Yes, it is.'

'When did they meet?'

'Lucy came into the Cairns office to see me and they clicked. Simple as that,' she said airily.

'And Harry, of course, met you when he went to see Mickey.'

'Yes.'

Realising that Elizabeth was not about to be chatty, Sarah backed off, only tossing out the comment, 'Well, it's all very interesting,' as she left the office.

It wasn't interesting so much as complicated, Elizabeth thought. She didn't know if these connections were likely to lead anywhere good for either Lucy or herself. Two brothers who were close, two sisters who were close, the work situation—if things started going wrong, there could be a nasty ripple effect.

She remembered Lucy's blithe comment when Harry had been ordering their cocktails last Monday—*wouldn't it be great if we ended up together...all happy families!* Possibly it could be great if it worked out like that but Elizabeth wasn't counting on it. It was far too early to think the possibility was high.

Lucy slid out of relationships almost as fast as she started them.

As for herself and Harry, she couldn't even call it a relationship yet. All she could really say for certain was that her stance against him had been substantially shifted. And he was fantastic in bed!

It was almost midday when he called from the jetty to say Mickey's motor-launch was about to dock. Her nerves instantly started jangling, mocking any idea that she could breeze through this meeting with no angst at all. She fiercely told herself the important thing was to keep her composure, regardless of what she was feeling.

Lucy was hugging Michael's arm when Harry led them into the office—the woman in possession and obviously loving having this man in tow. Her skin was glowing, her eyes were shining and the smile on her face beamed brilliant happiness. Elizabeth's heart contracted at this evidence that her sister was over-the-moon in love.

'This island is fabulous, Ellie,' she cried. 'What a great place to work!'

'Tropical paradise,' Elizabeth responded, pasting a smile on her face and moving from behind the desk to greet them appropriately.

Lucy released Michael's arm to rush forward and give her a hug. 'Are you loving it?' she asked, her eyes bright with curiosity about the situation, which, of course, included Harry.

'Not too much, I hope,' Michael semi-growled in the background.

'It's been quite a change,' she said dryly, flicking him a sharply assessing look.

Somehow he was more handsome than ever, his face relaxed in a friendly way, his very male physique shown off in casual clothes—smartly tailored shorts in a blue-and-grey check teamed with a royal blue sports shirt. He still had the impact of an alpha man scoring ten out of ten, but she wasn't feeling it so personally anymore. He belonged to her sister now.

'A good one, I hope,' Harry slid in, drawing her attention to him.

Another alpha man—no doubt about it now—and the memory of last night's intimacy caused a wave of warm pleasure to roll through her. The piercing blue eyes were digging at her again, but she didn't resent it this time. He *cared* about what she was feeling.

'Yes,' she answered with a smile, wanting to allay his concern for her.

'Now, Harry, poaching my PA is not on,' Michael shot at him.

'Like I said before, Mickey—*her choice*,' he replied with an affable shrug.

'Okay, while you two guys argue over my brilliant sister, I want her to show me her living quarters,' Lucy put in quickly. 'You can mind the office, can't you, Harry?'

'Go right ahead,' he said agreeably.

'Come on, Ellie,' she urged, nodding to the door at the back of the office. 'Michael said your apartment was right here. I want to see everything. And while I'm at it, may I say you look great in the island uniform?'

Elizabeth laughed. 'Not as spectacular as you this morning.'

Lucy wore cheeky little navy denim shorts with a red-and-purple halter top, big red hoop earrings, red trainers on her feet and a purple scrunchie holding up her long blond hair in a ponytail.

'Am I over-the-top?' she asked.

Elizabeth shook her head. 'You can carry off anything, Lucy.'

'I wish…' she replied with a wry grimace as Elizabeth ushered her into the apartment and closed the door on the two men in the office.

Elizabeth eyed her quizzically, sensing something was weighing on her sister's mind. 'Is that a general wish or…?'

'Oh, nothing really,' came the airy reply, her hands gesturing dismissively as her gaze swung around the living room. 'This is lovely, Ellie. Show me the bedroom and bathroom.'

She stopped at the queen-size bed, her sherry-brown eyes twinkling mischief at Elizabeth. 'Have you shared this with Harry yet?'

'Actually, no.' Wanting to divert any further personal probing, she retaliated with, 'Do you want to tell me what's going on with Michael?'

She threw up her hands. 'Everything is happening! I swear to you, Ellie, I've never been this mad about a guy. I'm in love like you wouldn't believe, and while it's incredibly wonderful, it's also scary, you know?'

'In what way scary?'

She flopped onto the bed, put her hands behind her head and stared at the ceiling. 'Michael is smart. I mean *really* smart, isn't he?'

'Yes.'

'So what happens when he finds out that my brain wasn't wired right and I'm a dummy when it comes to reading and writing? So far I've been winging it as I usually do, but this is far more intense than it's been with other guys, and he's bound to start noticing I'm a bit weird about some things.' She rolled her head to look straight at Elizabeth, a yearning appeal in her eyes. 'You've worked for him for two years. Will it put him off me if I tell him I'm dyslexic?'

Having experienced how exacting he was about everything to do with work, Elizabeth could only answer, 'I honestly don't know, Lucy. Does it feel as though he's in love with you?'

'Well, definitely in lust.' Her forehead puckered. 'I can't be sure that's love, but I really want it to be, Ellie. More than I've wanted anything. I want him to care so much about having me, it won't matter that I'm flawed.'

Elizabeth sat on the bed beside her and smoothed the worried furrows from her brow. 'It shouldn't matter if he loves you. And stop thinking of yourself as a dummy, Lucy. You're very smart, and you have so many talents…any man would be lucky to have you in his life.'

She heaved a rueful sigh. 'Well, I don't want him to know yet. I couldn't bear it if…' Her eyes shot a pleading look at Elizabeth. 'You haven't told Harry, have you?'

'No. And I won't.'

'I need more time. To give it a chance, you know?'

'Yes, I know.'

'I've been running off at the mouth about me. What about you and Harry?'

Elizabeth shrugged. 'Same thing. More time needed.'

'But you do like him.'

'Yes.' The hostility towards him had completely dissipated last night, as had the steaming vexation and resentment he had so frequently stirred. As it was now, there was nothing not to like.

Lucy propped herself on her elbow, an earnest expression on her face. 'Promise me you won't go off him if things don't work out between me and Michael.'

She hadn't expected Lucy, who had always seemed to be a live-in-the-moment person, to look ahead and see complications arising from the situation. It took her by surprise. Before she could consider the promise, Lucy rattled on.

'Harry could be the right guy for you. Let's face it…he's gorgeous and sexy and wealthy and obviously keen to have you in his corner. You could be great together and I don't want *me* to be the reason for you not having a future with him. I'd be happy to see you happy with him, Ellie, regardless of what happens between me and Michael.'

Deeply touched by her sister's caring, she couldn't help replying, 'But being so madly in love with Michael, you'll be hurt if he walks away from you.' Just as *she* had been on Monday—totally shattered and never wanting to see him again.

'Oh, I'll muddle along like I always do,' Lucy retorted with a wry grimace. 'I'm good at putting things behind me. I've had a lot of practice at it.' She reached out, took Elizabeth's hand and squeezed it reassuringly. 'You mustn't worry about me. Go for what you want. You deserve a good life, Ellie.'

'So do you.'

'Well, maybe we'll both achieve it. Who knows? I just want to clear the deck for you and Harry. Now tell me you're okay with that.'

Elizabeth heaved a sigh to relieve the heavy emotional fullness in her chest and finally said, 'I'm okay if you're okay.' She squeezed her sister's hand back. 'Whatever happens with either of us, we'll always have each other, Lucy.'

'Absolutely!' she agreed, the earnestness breaking into a wide grin. 'Now let's go get our men!' She bounced off the bed and twirled around in a happy dance. 'Let's have a fabulous weekend, following our hearts' desire and not thinking about tomorrow.' She paused in the doorway to the living room to give Elizabeth a wise look. 'You never know when something might strike us dead so we do what we want to do. Right?'

'Right!' Elizabeth echoed, suddenly wondering how much of Lucy's attitudes and behaviour stemmed from their mother's early death and the suffering that had preceded it.

She'd only been seventeen. Would Michael wrap her in the loving security blanket she needed? It was simply impossible to know at this point.

When she and Lucy emerged from the apartment, the two men were still standing where they'd left them in the office. Michael's attention instantly swivelled away from Harry, his face lighting up with pleasure at seeing her sister again. He held out his arms in a welcome-back gesture and Lucy waltzed straight into them, laughing up at him as she curled her arms around his neck.

'All done here?' he asked indulgently.

'Yes. But I want all four of us to lunch together in the restaurant.'

He threw a quick appeal to his brother. 'That can be arranged?'

'Leave it with me,' Harry said, not exactly committing to the idea. 'Why don't you take Lucy across to the restaurant, order a bottle of wine, and we'll join you when we've cleared the way?'

'See you soon,' Lucy tossed at Elizabeth as Michael scooped her away with him.

Which left her alone with Harry.

She'd been watching Michael very intently, wishing she could see into his mind and heart, knowing now that he could hurt Lucy very badly if lust didn't turn into love. This wasn't another flash-in-the-pan attraction for her—easy come, easy go.

Was he *the right man* for her sister?

A little while ago she had believed he was the perfect match for herself. It was hard to get her head around transferring that sense of *rightness* to the connection between Michael and Lucy, but at least it didn't hurt anymore. She felt no jealousy. No envy. Just a rather horrid sense that fate was playing a capricious trick in seeding attractions with the potential to mess up their lives.

Harry clenched his hands in instinctive fighting mode. Throughout the whole encounter with Mickey and Lucy, Elizabeth's attention had been trained on them. She hadn't looked to him for any help. Even now with them gone, her focus was inward, probably measuring her feelings and unwilling to reveal them.

Was she still obsessed with Mickey?

He needed to know.

'Elizabeth…' he said more tersely than he'd meant to.

Her gaze flicked up to his. He saw no pain

in her eyes. It was more a look of curious assessment. *Of him.* Was she comparing what she'd felt for Mickey with how she now felt about him? Last night's intimacy had to have had some impact on her. She'd responded to him very positively.

'If you'd rather not have lunch with them…' he started, willing to make up some excuse for her to avoid spending more time in their company if she found it intolerable.

'No, it's fine,' she cut in. 'If it's okay with you for me to vacate the office for the lunch hour.'

'You're sure?' he asked, wanting absolute confirmation that she was free of any angst over her sister's connection with his brother.

A whimsical smile softened her expression as she walked towards him. To his surprise and delight, when she reached him she slid her hands up his chest and linked them around the back of his neck. 'Lucy said to go get our men and right now you're my man, Harry. I hope you're happy about that,' she said in a soft seductive lilt.

Was it true?

He fiercely didn't want it to be on the rebound.

He wrapped his arms around her and

pulled her into full body contact with him. No resistance. In fact, she rubbed herself teasingly against him, stirring an instant erection. Her eyes blazed with a boldness he'd never seen in them and he sensed a determination in her to take life by the scruff of the neck and give it a good shake.

Whatever... Her dream about Mickey was gone and she was choosing to have him. He kissed her and she kissed him right back, no hesitation, no inhibitions—a full-blooded response that made it extremely difficult to rein in the desire she'd fired up. It was the wrong time to race her off to bed. Mickey and Lucy were waiting for them in the restaurant and he wouldn't put it past Lucy to come looking for them if they didn't appear within a reasonable time.

Besides, the promise was certainly there that last night was not going to be the one-night stand Elizabeth had dictated.

He could wait.

He was satisfied that he'd won.

Elizabeth Flippence was now *his* woman.

CHAPTER FOURTEEN

ELIZABETH woke up on Sunday morning and was instantly aware of the man lying in the bed he hadn't shared with her before last night—the sound of his breathing, the warmth emanating from his naked body, the memories of intense pleasure in their love-making. Harry Finn...

She rolled onto her back to look at him, a smile twitching at her lips. He was still asleep. Her gaze wandered over every part of him that was not covered by the bed sheet—the strongly muscled shoulders and arms, the ruggedly masculine face with its slightly crooked nose, the black curls flopping over his forehead, the five o'clock shadow on his jaw. *Her man*, she thought, at least for the time being.

It felt slightly weird but definitely liber-ating to have thrown out her rule book on how life should be led, diving straight into the deep end with Harry and not caring if it was a big mistake. Lucy's comment yesterday—*you never know when something might strike us dead so we do what we want to do*—had made it seem stupid to deny herself what Harry could give her out of fear that she'd made a rash choice and this lovely time with him probably wouldn't last.

So what if it didn't!

She was thirty years old. Why not experience all the pleasure she could with this man? When—*if*—it ended, at least she would have had the most marvellous sex any woman could have.

She wondered if Lucy was feeling the same about Michael. Was he as good a lover as his brother? Did being *in love* make it better? It was far too soon to say she was in love with Harry but he was much—*nicer*—than she had ever thought he could be, not like a superficial playboy at all. He really did care about her feelings.

His eyes suddenly flicked open, instantly catching her looking at him. 'Hi!' he said, his mouth curving into a happy smile.

She smiled back. 'Hi to you, too!'

'How long have you been awake?'

She reached out and ran a finger down his nose. 'Long enough to wonder how this got broken.'

He laughed and rolled onto his side, propping himself up on his elbow, answering her good-humouredly. 'Rugby tackle. It made a bloody mess of my nose but I stopped the other guy from scoring a try and we won the game.'

'Sport,' she said, mentally correcting her former prejudice that had decided the injury had come out of a misspent youth. 'Jack Pickard told me you'd been good at all sports in your teens. He reckoned you could have been a champion on any playing field.'

He cocked an eyebrow at her. 'You were asking him about me?'

'No. I was being told about you. But I am asking now. Tell me about those years, Harry. What were your proudest moments in sport?'

He was happy to talk about them, basking in her interest. For two years she had rejected knowing more about him, always projecting the attitude that he wasn't worth knowing. That glacier of disinterest had definitely thawed over the past two days.

'Did you ever dream of competing in the

Olympic Games? Or representing Australia in rugby or cricket?' she asked.

He shook his head. 'I simply enjoyed sport. I never aimed to make a career out of it. Mickey and I wanted to join Dad in the business. He used to talk to us about what he was doing, what he was planning. It was creative, challenging, exciting....' He grinned. 'And you made your own rules, no toeing a line drawn for you by sport officialdom.'

'You were lucky to have a father like that, Harry.'

Not like hers.

He saw it in her eyes, heard it in the tinge of sad envy in her voice. He remembered what she had told him about her own father and realised how cautious she would be about her relationships with men, judging them on character before allowing them into her life. Playboy—womaniser—that would be a firm no-no regardless of physical attraction. No doubt she would instantly back off from anyone showing a bent towards drinking too much alcohol, as well.

A very strong-minded woman.

Her sister's anchor.

She'd been a challenge to him and he hadn't looked any further than winning her over, having her like this, but he found himself wanting to prove she was safe with him. He was not one of the bad guys.

'I'm going to be the same kind of father to my children,' he said firmly.

It raised her eyebrows. 'You see a future with a family in it?'

'Yes, I do. Don't you?'

She looked uncertain. 'I don't know anymore. I feel a bit adrift at the moment, Harry.'

She had probably dreamed of it with Mickey and that dream was gone. He understood her sense of being adrift. He didn't know how deep it went until much later in the day.

Lunch with Lucy and Michael again before they headed back to the mainland. Elizabeth felt no stress about joining them. She wanted to observe how well they were responding to each other, watch for any pricks in their bubble of happiness. It troubled her that Lucy saw her dyslexia as a possible breaking point. She wished she could have given her sister an assurance that it wouldn't be.

It was a problem, no denying it. She suspected it played a big part in Lucy's flightiness, why relationships and jobs never lasted long. It wasn't a happy position—being thought defective. If Michael ever did think it and rejected her sister on that basis, Elizabeth knew she would hate him for it.

As soon as they were all seated in the restaurant and handed menus with the limited list of four starters, four mains and four sweets, Elizabeth mused over all of them out loud so Lucy could make her choice without having to say she'd have the same as someone else. Often in restaurants a waiter listed Specials which made a selection easy, but that wasn't the case here.

Lucy grinned at her, eyes sparkling gratitude, and it was obvious that nothing had changed between her and Michael. They still looked besotted with each other, and the meal progressed in a very congenial atmosphere.

Until they were sitting over coffee at the end of it.

'Any prospects for the position of manager here, Harry?' Michael asked.

He shrugged. 'A few résumés have come in. I haven't called for any interviews yet. Elizabeth may want to stay on now that she's on top of the job.'

'Elizabeth is mine!' Michael shot at him with a vexed look.

'No!' tripped straight out of her mouth.

The vexed look was instantly transferred to her. 'Don't tell me Harry has seduced you into staying here.'

'No, I won't be staying here beyond the month he needs to find someone suitable.'

As beautiful as the island was, it was a getaway, too isolated from a normal social life for her to stay on indefinitely, too far away from Lucy, too. Besides, if the affair with Harry ran cold, she'd feel trapped here.

'So you come back to me,' Michael insisted.

She shook her head. 'I'm sorry, Michael, but I don't want to do that, either.'

Being his PA wasn't a straightforward work situation anymore. The personal connections that had started this week—him and Lucy, herself and Harry—made it too emotionally complicated for her to feel comfortable about working closely with him.

'Why not?' he persisted.

She was acutely aware of Lucy listening and needed to dissuade her sister from thinking it was because of her. 'Being here this week made me realise I want a change. Try something different. I'd appreciate it if you'd take this as my notice, Michael.'

He wasn't happy. He glared at his brother. 'Goddammit, Harry! If it wasn't for you…'

'Hey!' Harry held up his hands defensively. 'I'm not getting her, either.'

'Please…' Elizabeth quickly broke in, feeling the rise of tension around the table. 'I don't want to cause trouble. I just want to take a different direction with my life.'

'But you're brilliant as my PA,' Michael argued, still annoyed at being put out.

'I'm sorry. You'll just have to find someone else.'

She wasn't about to budge from this stance. It felt right to divorce herself from both the Finn men as far as work was concerned. Whatever developed in a personal sense had to be something apart from professional ties, not tangled up with how she earned her income.

'Why not try out Lucy as your PA?' Harry suggested to Michael with an airy wave of his hand. 'She's probably as brilliant as her sister.'

Lucy looked aghast, panic in her eyes.

'It's not her kind of thing,' Elizabeth said firmly.

Michael frowned and turned to her sister. 'You do work in administration, Lucy,' he remarked quizzically.

'I'm the front person who deals with people, Michael,' she rushed out. 'I don't do the desk work. I'm good at helping people, understanding what they want, helping them to decide…there's quite a bit of that in cemetery administration. And I like it,' she added for good measure, pleading for him to drop the issue.

He grimaced, accepting that Lucy was no easy solution to his problem.

She reached out and touched his hand, desperate to restore his good humour with her. 'I'm sorry I can't fill Ellie's place.'

The grimace tilted up into a soothing smile. 'I shouldn't have expected it. You are a people person and I like that, Lucy. I wouldn't want to change it.'

Elizabeth saw relief pouring through the smile beamed back at him. Another hurdle safely jumped, she thought. Yet hiding the dyslexia from Michael couldn't go on forever and there was one thing she needed from him before the situation could get horribly messed up.

'I hope you'll give me a good reference, Michael.'

He sighed and turned a rueful smile to her. 'It will be in the mail tomorrow. I hate losing you but I wish you well, Elizabeth.'

'Thank you.'

Harry didn't like Elizabeth's decision any more than Mickey did. She was cutting ties with them, closing doors, and he didn't know her reasons for it. This morning he could have sworn she was over her emotional fixation on his brother but if that was true, why give up her job with him? It was a top-line position and on the salary front Harry doubted she could better it.

He had offered her an alternative but she wasn't taking up that option. It was understandable that staying on the island long-term would not suit her. She and her sister lived together and were obviously close—family who really counted as family, like him and Mickey. Apart from that, if she wanted to re-join the social swing, Cairns was the place to do it.

He didn't like this thought, either. It meant she didn't see much of a future with him, which raised the question in his mind—how much of a future did he want with her?

She touched places in him that no other woman had, but did he do the same to her? More time together should sort that out, but there was one thing he needed to know right now because it was twisting up his gut.

Was she still using him to fight off her feelings for Mickey?

Elizabeth silently fretted over whether she had spoken her mind too soon, aware that her announcements had upset the happy mood around the table. Although Michael had accepted her decision on the surface, it was obvious from the stony glances he threw at Harry that he blamed his brother for it and was barely holding in his frustration over the situation. Her nerves picked up tension emanating from Harry. Lucy kept looking anxiously at her. No one chose to eat any of the petit fours that accompanied coffee.

As soon as Elizabeth had finished her cappuccino, Lucy pushed back her chair and rose to her feet. 'I'm off to the ladies' room. Will you come with me, Ellie?' Her eyes begged agreement.

'Of course,' she said, immediately rising to join her sister.

The barrage started the moment they were closeted in the ladies' room. 'Why are you leaving your great job with Michael? He's not happy about it.'

Elizabeth shook her head. 'It's not my mission in life to keep Michael happy,' she said dryly.

'But you always said you loved that job.'

'I did, but it's high pressure, Lucy. I didn't realise how much it demanded of me until I came out here. I don't want to be constantly on my toes anymore. I want to look for something else—more relaxed, less stressful.'

'Then it's not because of me and him?' she said worriedly.

'No,' Elizabeth lied. 'I'm sorry Michael is unhappy about it but I don't think he'll take it out on you, Lucy. If he does, he's not the man for you.'

She heaved a sigh. 'You're right. Okay. It's completely fair for you to look for something else. He's just got to lump being put out by it.'

'You can play nurse and soothe his frustration,' Elizabeth said with a smile.

Lucy laughed.

It eased the tension on that front.

However, Michael's displeasure with her decision made the farewells after lunch somewhat strained. Elizabeth hoped that Lucy's company would be bright enough to move his annoyance aside. She hadn't meant to spoil their day.

Harry followed her into the administration office, obviously intent on pursuing the issue of her leaving his employ, as well, although he shouldn't have any grievance with her. She had only ever agreed to the month needed for him to find another manager.

Wanting to clear that deck, she swung around to face him, quickly saying, 'I won't stay on, Harry. I didn't promise to.'

His grim expression surprised her. The laser-blue eyes were so hard and piercing, her heart jumped into a gallop. The air between them seemed to gather an intensity that played havoc with her nerves.

'Why did you throw in your job with Mickey?' he shot at her.

'I explained why,' she said defensively.

'You waffled to whitewash the true reason,' he accused. 'Tell me, Elizabeth.'

He had no right to delve into her private reading of a highly personal situation for herself and her sister. It was not his business. It was the involvement with his brother that was the problem and she was not about to spell that out.

'I'm sorry you thought it was waffle.' She shrugged. 'I don't know what else to say.'

His mouth thinned in frustration. He shook his head at her refusal to open up to him. 'I knew you were using me on Friday night,' he stated bitingly. 'That whole scenario at the pavilion villa was more about Michael and Lucy than being with me. I want to know if what you've done with me since then and what you decided today was also driven by your feelings for my brother.'

Her face flamed with shame at how she had used him and her mind jammed with shock that he could believe she was still doing it. 'No!' she cried, forcing her feet forward to go to him, her eyes pleading forgiveness for her brutal lack of caring for *his* feelings. 'I don't even think of Michael anymore, not with any wanting in my mind or heart,' she said vehemently. 'I haven't been using you, Harry. Even on Friday night I was confused about why I was doing what I did with you.'

She reached him and laid her hands on his chest, meeting his scouring gaze with open honesty. 'Since then, I swear I've enjoyed every minute with you, wanting to know the person you are, liking what I'm learning about you. Please don't think any of it was related to your brother.'

He frowned, not yet appeased by her outcry. 'Then why not work for Mickey?'

She grimaced at his persistence. 'Maybe I just don't want to be reminded of how silly I was. A break is better, Harry.' She slid her hands up around his neck and pressed her body to his, craving the wild warmth and excitement of his desire again. 'Can we forget about Michael now? Please?'

His eyes still scoured hers for the truth. His hands gripped her waist hard as though he was in two minds whether to pull her closer or push her away. 'He's my brother,' he said gruffly.

And Lucy was her sister, whom Michael could hurt very badly.

'Does that mean I *have* to work for him or I'll lose any interest you have in me, Harry?'

Again his brow beetled down. 'That's not the point.'

'Good! Because as much as I want what you and I are having together, I won't let any man dictate how I lead my life.'

That was a core truth.

She wanted a partner in life, not a lord and master.

Harry believed her. There was a strength in this woman that had always challenged him. As much as it had frustrated him in the past, he admired the way she made a decision and stuck to it. A warrior woman, he thought wryly, one who would fight tooth and nail for what she believed was right.

Yet she was vulnerable to the womanly needs that he'd tapped into. The wanting for him was in the soft giving of her body appealing to his, the hand-lock at the back of his neck, the slight pouting of her mouth waiting for a kiss that would blow everything else away. The challenge in her eyes burned into his brain. She was his for the taking, not Mickey's, and the compulsion to take her forced him to set all reservations aside.

He kissed her.

She kissed him back.

And Harry revelled in the sense that this was a true beginning of a relationship that promised to be more *right* than any he had known.

CHAPTER FIFTEEN

ELIZABETH managed the administration office on her own throughout her second week on Finn Island. She didn't feel lonely. There were daily meetings with Sarah and Jack Pickard and Daniel Marven. Apart from them, many of the guests dropped by to chat about what they'd done or what they planned to do while they were here. Quite a few were much-travelled tourists from other countries, who couldn't resist comparing this place to other getaways they had enjoyed, always favourably, which Elizabeth thought was a feather in Harry's cap.

He'd carried through his vision for this resort with an attention to detail that was every bit as meticulous as Michael's in his side of the business. In that respect he was just as solid as his brother. In fact, he really had none of the characteristics of a playboy who cared little for anything except indulging himself with passing pleasures.

He called her each day to check on how she was doing and they had quite long conversations that always left her smiling. Contact with him didn't make her tense anymore. They discussed many things with an ease that she thoroughly enjoyed. Even the flirtatious remarks that she'd once hated, once left her steaming with anger, now made her laugh and spread a delicious warmth through her body.

It continually amazed her how much her life had changed in such a short amount of time. Giving up the Michael dream that had been gnawing at her for so long and giving in to the attraction Harry had always exerted on her…it was as though a whole lot of inner conflict had been lifted from her. She had set aside worries about the future, letting herself be a happy butterfly. When serious issues had to be faced, she would face them. But that wasn't yet.

Emails from Lucy were full of dizzy pleasure with her love affair with Michael. According to her sister, he was everything wonderful. Still early days, Elizabeth thought, but hoped the relationship would become what both of them were looking for to complement their lives. And who knew... maybe Harry might turn out to be the right partner for her?

He returned to the island on Saturday morning, strolling into the office, a wide grin on his face, eyes sparkling with pleasure at seeing her again. Her heart jumped. Her feet jumped. She was out of her chair, wanting to skip around the desk and hurl herself at him, driven by a wild eagerness to revel in all the sexual excitement his physical presence instantly aroused in her. Only a sense of decorum held her back. Or rather a very basic female instinct to have him demonstrate his desire for her first.

Her smile, however, was an open invitation to take up where he'd left off last weekend. 'Hi!' she said in a breathy rush.

He strode forward, dumped the attaché case he was carrying on the desk and swept her into his embrace. 'Can't wait another minute,' he said and kissed her with a hunger that ignited the same hunger in her.

It was great to feel so wanted.

What made the physical sizzle between them even better was the respect he subsequently showed for her opinion. He'd brought the résumés of the most likely prospects for the position of manager with him and wanted her input on them before deciding on interviews. This sharing on a business level made Elizabeth feel like a real partner, not just for sharing a bed.

They talked about the possibilities for most of the day, weighing up the pros and cons, deciding on who would best deal with the situation. There seemed to be a wonderful, vibrant harmony flowing between them, making their lovemaking that night extra special. It wasn't until Harry chose to query her choices that the pleasurable flow was broken.

They were lying face to face, their legs still intimately locked together. Harry softly stroked the feathery bangs off her forehead, looking deeply into her eyes. 'I'd really like you to stay on here, Ellie,' he said. 'It's not too late to change your mind.'

Her chest instantly grew tight. It was difficult to resist the seductive pressure of his words when she wanted to cling onto the sweet sense of everything being perfect. 'I can't, Harry,' she blurted out.

He frowned at her quick reply. 'You've been happy here this past week. I've heard it in your voice every time I've called. And today you've been so relaxed, confident. Why not reconsider?'

'It's better that you get someone else,' she argued.

'But I like feeling you're part of my world, Ellie. It's been great this week, sharing it with you.'

She sucked in a deep breath, needing to hold firm against the persuasive pull of a future that might mean sharing his world forever. It was too soon to know, her mind screamed, too soon to commit to the possibility. She reached up and stroked his cheek, her eyes pleading for understanding.

'I'm not rejecting you, Harry. I just need to be where Lucy is. Being on this island in a permanent position is too far away.'

He heaved a sigh, his mouth turning into a wry grimace. 'You have to be there for her.'

'Yes.'

'Well, I guess I'll just have to invade your world in Cairns.'

She relaxed at his acceptance of her decision, smiling as she said, 'I hope you do.'

Harry told himself to be content with her apparent willingness to continue their relationship once she was back in Cairns. Separating herself from both Mickey and himself professionally had niggled at him. She'd been so elusive in the past, he wasn't absolutely confident that he'd won her over into moving forward with him.

They'd certainly gone beyond a one-night stand and he no longer thought this was a rebound situation. The connection between them was too good to doubt it. Still, the fact that she was severing the work connection… Harry shook it out of his mind. There was no point in letting it throw a cold shadow over the warmth of their intimacy tonight.

He had her where he wanted her.

It was enough for now.

The call-tune on his mobile phone woke him to the dim light of dawn.

Elizabeth stirred, as well, asking, 'Who'd be wanting to contact you at this hour?'

'Don't know,' he muttered, hoping it wasn't bad trouble of some sort as he rolled out of bed and retrieved the mobile from his shorts pocket. He quickly flipped it open, held it up to his ear and spoke a terse, 'Yes?'

'Harry Finn?' asked a male voice he didn't recognise.

'Yes. Who's speaking?'

'This is Constable Colin Parker. I'm calling from the Cairns Base Hospital. I'm sorry to say your brother, Michael Finn, was involved in a serious car accident earlier this morning....'

Harry's heart stopped. Shock and fear jammed his mind for a moment, fear spearing through to force out the words, 'How serious?'

'Your brother and two teenagers are in intensive care. I can't say exactly what injuries were sustained but I'm told they are extensive. Two other teenagers...'

'He's not dead.' Relief poured through Harry. Although there was no guarantee Mickey would pull through, at least he had a chance, not like their parents.

'Who?' Elizabeth cried, alarmed by what she'd heard.

It instantly recalled the high probability that Lucy had been with Mickey—a Saturday night—out on the town. 'Was my brother alone in his car?'

Elizabeth clapped her hands to her face, her eyes wide with horror, a gasp of shock leaving her mouth open.

'Yes, he was. No passengers.'

'Lucy wasn't with him,' he swiftly assured

her. 'Thank you for letting me know, Constable. I'll get to the hospital as soon as I can.'

He grabbed his clothes and headed straight for the bathroom, his mind racing over which would be the fastest way to the mainland. Calling for a helicopter, getting the pilot out of bed and to the airfield—no, he couldn't bear waiting around. Best to take the yacht back to Cairns at full throttle, be on the move. He could easily summon a car to meet him at the marina, drive him straight to the hospital, no time wasted.

You hang on, Mickey, he fiercely willed his brother.

Elizabeth had wrapped a robe around her and was pacing the bedroom floor when he emerged from the bathroom. 'How bad is it?' she shot at him, anguish in her eyes.

It made Harry think she still cared a hell of a lot for his brother, which put another savage twist in his heart.

Her hands lifted in urgent plea. 'Lucy will want to know.'

Anguish for her sister or herself? He shook his head. He didn't have time to sort this out. 'He's in intensive care. That's all the cop could tell me,' he answered. 'I have to go now, Elizabeth. Will you hold on here until…

until…' He couldn't bring himself to voice whatever was going to happen.

'Of course I will,' she cried. 'I'll do anything you want me to do. Just call me. I'll stand by as long as you need me.'

Yes, Harry thought. *The one who had always carried the load. Always would. The anchor.*

He walked over to her, scooped her into a tight embrace, needing a brief blast of warmth to take some of the chill out of his bones. He rubbed his cheek over her silky hair and kissed the top of her head. 'Thank you. I'll be in touch,' he murmured, then set her aside to go to his brother.

Elizabeth was not going to leave him any day soon.

Mickey might.

Elizabeth's heart bled for him as she watched him make a fast exit from her apartment. To have his parents killed in an accident and now to have his brother on the danger list from another accident…it was a wickedly unkind twist of fate.

When she had thought Lucy could be involved, too… The huge relief at hearing she wasn't made her feel guilty for being spared what Harry was going through—totally gutted with fear and anxiety. It was no empty promise that she would do anything to help. If she had the power to make everything better for him, she would. He was a good man.

So was Michael.

And Lucy would want to know that the man she loved was in hospital, possibly fighting for his life.

Where was her sister? Why hadn't she been with Michael? Had there been a bust-up between them? Questions fired through Elizabeth's mind as she used her mobile phone to make contact with her. The call tone went on for a long nerve-tearing time before it was finally cut off by Lucy's voice, sounding groggy with sleep.

Of course, it was still very early in the morning—Sunday morning—but time didn't matter. 'Wake up, Lucy!' she said sharply. 'There's been an accident.'

'What? Is that you, Ellie?'

'Yes. Michael was injured in a car accident early this morning. He was badly hurt.'

'Michael…oh, no…no…' It was a wail of anguished protest. 'Oh, God! It's my fault!'

'How is it your fault?'

'I ate something at dinner last night that

upset me. He brought me home. I was vomiting and had dreadful diarrhoea. He left me to find an all-night pharmacy, get me some medicine. I was so drained I must have drifted off to sleep. He should have come back but he's not here and… Oh, God! He went out for me, Ellie!'

'Stop that, Lucy! You didn't cause the accident and getting hysterical won't help Michael,' she said vehemently, needing to cut off the futile guilt trip. 'I take it everything was still good between you last night?'

'Yes…yes…he was so caring when I was sick. Oh, Ellie! I'll die if I lose him.'

'Then you'd better do whatever you can to make him want to live. Are you still sick? Can you get to the hospital? He's in an intensive care unit.'

'I'll get there.' Gritty determination was in her voice, hysteria gone.

'Harry was with me on the island. He's on his way. Be kind to him, Lucy. Remember he and Michael lost their parents in an accident. I have to stay here. Harry's counting on me to take care of business but I think he'll need someone there, too.'

'I understand. You love him but you can't be with him.'

Love? That was typical Lucy. Elizabeth cared about the man and she certainly loved aspects of him, but she mentally shied from putting a boots-and-all love tag on her feelings for Harry. However, right at this moment it was easier to just let her sister think what she wanted to think.

'I need to know what's happening, Lucy. Please…will you keep me informed?'

'Sure! I'll call you with news as soon as I have it. Moving now. Over and out. Okay?'

'Okay.'

Elizabeth took a long deep breath, trying to settle some of her inner agitation. There was no more she could do about the situation, yet the need for some kind of action was twitching through her nerves. The office didn't have to be opened for hours yet. It was too early for anyone on the island to require her for anything.

She showered and dressed, then walked down to the beach, dropping onto a deckchair to simply sit and watch the sunrise, wanting to feel some peace with a world that had just changed again. Nature kept rolling on, regardless of what happened to human beings. While it could be ugly, too—cyclones, floods, droughts—this morning it had a beautiful tranquillity that soothed the turmoil in her soul.

The sea was a glittering expanse of shimmering wavelets. The sky slowly turned into a pastel panorama of pinks and lemons. The sun crept up over the horizon, shooting beams of light into the tinted clouds. It was a lovely dawning of a new day—another day that she was *alive*.

Life was precious.

More than ever Elizabeth felt a pressing need to make the most of it.

This past week with Harry had been good.

She'd felt happy with him.

Love was a big step from there but her mind and heart were opening up to the chance that Harry Finn might be the man who could and would share her life in all the ways she'd dreamed of.

CHAPTER SIXTEEN

ELIZABETH was on tenterhooks all morning waiting for news of Michael. She thought it would be Lucy who called, but it was Harry, instantly assuring her that his brother's injuries were not life-threatening as they had feared.

'He was hit on the driver's side, right arm and hip fractured, broken ribs, lacerations to the face, a lot of bruising, concussion. The doctors were worried that a broken rib had punctured his liver but that's been cleared and bones will mend.' His sigh transmitted a mountain of relief. 'He's going to be incapacitated for quite a while, but there should be no lasting damage.'

'That's good news, Harry,' Elizabeth said, her own relief pouring into her voice.

'Lucy's here. I've left her sitting beside

Mickey, holding his left hand. She's certainly a surprise, your sister.'

'What do you mean?'

'He's not a pretty picture—face cut, bruised and swollen. I didn't think it was a good idea, her going in to see him. Thought she'd have hysterics or faint at the sight of him. She gave me an earbashing on how much she cared about Mickey and she was no wimp when it came to facing anyone who was suffering anything.'

Elizabeth smiled, imagining the scene. 'I told you she was good with Mum.'

'Looks like she'll be good with Mickey, too. Like Mum was with Dad. He'll need cheering up in the days to come, that's for sure. He's sedated right now. Haven't spoken to him, only to the doctors, who assure me he's out of the woods.'

'That's the important thing, Harry. Whatever the future brings, he does have a future.'

'Thank God!'

'How did the accident happen? Lucy said he'd left her to find an all-night pharmacy…'

'Drunken teenagers in a stolen car running a red light. They just slammed into him. All four of them are here in the hospital, undoubtedly ruing their stupid joy ride. I can't say I'm feeling any sympathy for them.'

Harsh words, but justified, Elizabeth thought. Nevertheless, concern for him made her ask, 'Are you okay, Harry? I know shock can hit hard and have lingering after-effects.'

He heaved another big sigh, releasing tension this time. 'I'll be fine. Got to step in for Mickey. I'll have to run the Cairns office until he can pick up the reins again. I can delegate the running of the tourist side for a while, but Mickey has always kept a very personal control of the franchises. There's no one I can hand it to.'

'I know,' she murmured understandingly, realising that his mind was racing, trying to foresee problems he had to deal with.

'I'll set up interviews with the two people we selected for the management position on the island, hopefully this week, then send the one I think is most appropriate out to you. If you'll train whomever I choose…'

'No problem,' she assured him. 'I'll get Sarah and Jack and Daniel to come on board for that, as well. We'll handle it for you, Harry. Don't worry about it. You'll have enough on your plate taking over from Michael. Just keep me informed on what's happening.'

'Will do. And thanks for…' He paused a moment, his voice gathering a husky note as he added, 'for being you, Elizabeth.'

The emotional comment brought a lump to her throat. It had been a stressful morning and she teetered on the edge of weeping now that the practicalities of the situation had been sorted out. She knew intuitively that Harry was close to breaking up, too, having held himself together to face the worst.

Having swallowed hard to clear her throat, she softly said, 'Don't be too alone in this, Harry. Anything you need to share…you can talk to me any time. Okay?'

Another pause, longer this time, making her wonder if she had stepped too far, assuming an intimacy he didn't feel with her when they weren't in bed together.

'Though I'm not into phone sex,' she blurted out.

He cracked up. Peal after peal of laughter sent her brain into a tizzy. She had no idea what it meant—a release from tension, amusement at her prudish restriction?

'Oh, Ellie! I love you,' he bubbled forth. 'I really, truly do.'

She was stunned into silence. Was this a genuine declaration or was he funning her?

'And it will kill me if you don't love me back,' he went on, slightly more soberly.

How was she to reply to that? 'Umm... Well, don't die any time soon, Harry.'

'I won't. I have too much to live for. And so do you, Ellie,' he said with conviction. 'Bye for now.'

Elizabeth didn't know what to think. In the end she decided Harry's *loving* her was simply an impulsive reaction to her helping him at a time of crisis. It was more comfortable putting it in that box than believing he was serious, because she didn't want to feel pressured about loving him back. As much as she liked him—maybe loved him—she wasn't ready to lay her heart completely on the line. It was too...*hasty*.

Harry knew he'd jumped the gun with the *love* words. They'd spilled out of him before he realised what he was saying, no consideration given to how they'd be received or interpreted and, worst of all, he couldn't *see* Elizabeth's reaction to them.

He'd spoken the truth. He knew that without any doubt now. The instinctive attraction had always been there and he'd never been able to give up on it, despite her constantly blocking it, preferring to see his brother as the more desirable man. But they were *right* together, *right* for each other. He felt it in his bones. Though he suspected she wasn't quite ready to hear or accept it.

Having given her word, she would still stand by him during this crisis. But until he was actually with her again, he'd steer clear of pouring out personal feelings. He wasn't absolutely sure that her emotions had been detached from his brother. Having sex with him—liking it, wanting it—that was certainly answering a need in her, but whether he'd won through to her heart was not certain at this point.

Patience, Harry, he cautioned himself.

Elizabeth Flippence was the woman worth keeping.

He had to convince her he was the man worth keeping.

Every day following Michael's accident, Elizabeth found herself literally hanging on calls from Cairns. She cared about Michael's progress—of course, she did—yet she grew impatient when Lucy went on endlessly about every little detail and her sympathy was sorely stretched at times. She really wanted to hear from Harry, not her sister.

Her heart always jumped when his voice came over the line and her body flooded with warm pleasure. Not once did he mention *loving* her, and despite thinking she didn't want to hear it, weirdly enough she actually did, although she was happy to simply chat with him and it felt really good to help him with problems he was encountering in Michael's office.

His confidence in her, his respect for her opinion, his desire for her input on everything, did touch her heart. Very deeply. None of her previous relationships with men had reached this level of sharing. She loved it. When he told her he was bringing his chosen candidate for manager over to the island himself at the weekend, she was thrilled at the prospect of being with him again, if only for a few hours.

He instructed her to hold a villa aside for herself from Saturday to the following Friday as the new manager would be taking over the apartment and she would probably need a week to ensure he was on top of the job. His name was David Markey and he was only twenty-eight, but he'd had experience as assistant manager at a resort on Kangaroo Island, which was down below Adelaide off the coast of South Australia. According to his résumé, he was keen to take up a position in a more tropical climate. Elizabeth had thought him a good possibility and she was glad he had interviewed well, leading Harry to choose him.

They were to arrive by helicopter on Saturday morning and the moment Elizabeth heard the distinctive noise of the rotors, her pulse started racing. She'd barely slept the night before, thinking of Harry and how it might be with him this time. It was difficult to contain the nervous excitement buzzing through her but somehow she had to keep it in check while she handled the business side of this visit.

Professionalism insisted that she couldn't run down to the back beach, waving madly like a child as the helicopter landed and flinging herself at Harry the moment he stepped out of it. Waiting in the office for the men to enter it was the right and sensible thing to do—the Elizabeth thing, she thought wryly, not the Lucy thing. But Harry was counting on her to be sensible and helpful. This was not *butterfly* time.

She'd asked Jack to meet the helicopter, introducing himself to David Markey as well as giving any help needed with luggage. While she waited, she forced herself to check through items laid out on her desk in preparation for making the job transition as easy as possible for David—a list of the current guests and the villas they occupied with a notation of activities some of them had booked today, contact numbers for the chef and the Pickards, a list of staff names under headings of housekeeping, maintenance and restaurant. It was all there waiting...waiting....

Harry led the others into the office. His vivid blue eyes connected with hers with such riveting intensity, Elizabeth was pinned to her chair while her heart rocketed around her chest. She stared back, feeling as though he was wrapping a magnetic field around her entire being, claiming her as his, tugging her towards him.

She stood. Her thighs were quivering, but her legs moved as though drawn by strings, drawn by the power of an attraction that had become totally irresistible. His smile bathed her in tingling pleasure. She was so con-

sumed by sheer awe at the strength of feelings shooting through her, the man moving
in beside Harry didn't register on her radar
until her attention was directed to him.

Harry lifted his hand in an introductory
wave, inclining his head towards the slightly
shorter man. 'David Markey, Elizabeth.'

'Good to meet you,' the newcomer
promptly said, stepping forward and extend-
ing his hand.

Elizabeth met it with her own hand, belat-
edly smiling a welcome. 'Likewise, David. I
hope you'll be very happy working here on
Finn Island.'

He was a clean-cut, good-looking young
man—short brown hair, bright brown eyes
with a ready smile to charm, a typical front
man in the hospitality industry. 'I'm very
glad to have the chance,' he said enthusias-
tically.

Jack had manoeuvred around the two men,
wheeling two suitcases towards the door into
the manager's apartment. Harry gestured towards him as he spoke to David. 'If you'll
just follow Jack, he'll show you your living
quarters and answer any questions you might
have about them. I want a private word with
Elizabeth.'

'Of course. Thank you,' was the ready reply, and taking the privacy hint, he closed the apartment door after himself.

The brief business with David had given Elizabeth enough distraction to recover from the initial impact of Harry's presence. Having regained some control of herself, she turned to him with a sympathetic smile. 'Tough week?'

'Mmm…' His eyes twinkled teasingly as he spread his arms in appeal. 'I think I need a hug.'

Her heart started racing again as she laughed and moved straight into his embrace, eager for the physical contact she had craved all week.

He hugged her tightly to him, rubbing his cheek against her hair, breathing in deeply and releasing a long, shuddering sigh before murmuring, 'There is nothing like a warm living body to make you feel better. I have so much wanted you with me this week, Ellie.'

'I wished I could have been there for you, too, Harry.'

'Can't be in two places at once,' he said wryly, tugging her head back so they were face to face. 'I'll stay here overnight if that's okay with you.'

'I was hoping you would,' she answered, openly showing that she welcomed every intimacy with him.

Desire blazed into his eyes. He lifted a hand and ran a feather-light finger over her lips. 'If I start kissing you I won't want to stop and there's no time for it now. When Jack comes out I'll leave you with David. Sarah wants me to lunch with them, hear all the news about Mickey firsthand. You should lunch with David in the restaurant, introduce him to the guests. I'll catch up with the two of you afterwards, find out how he's doing and hopefully get you to myself for a while.'

Assured they would be together later in the afternoon, Elizabeth didn't mind seeing Harry go off with Jack, happy with the plan of action he'd laid out. She knew how fond Sarah was of both the Finn brothers, and it was nice of Harry to answer the housekeeper's concern about Michael. It was also appropriate for her to introduce David to the guests since she was known to them, having been the resident manager all week.

Over lunch, David proved to have a very pleasant manner with the guests and the restaurant staff. Elizabeth quite enjoyed his company herself. He readily answered her questions about his experience on Kangaroo Island and was keen to question her experience at this resort, garnering as much knowledge as he could as quickly as he could.

It occurred to her that it might not take a week to fill him in on everything and make sure he understood the whole working process of the island. He wasn't coming in cold to the job as she had. He was already a professional in this field. It might only take a few days and then she could get back to Cairns.

To Lucy…

To Harry…

To real life again…

Although the island *getaway* hadn't really been a getaway for her. She'd been well and truly faced with real life here—forced to accept the reality of Michael's connection with Lucy, having her misconceptions about Harry ripped apart, learning that an attraction based on sexual chemistry could gather many more levels, given the chance.

Her time here had been one of intense emotional turmoil, yet coming now to the end of it, she was ready to move forward, wanting to move forward, hopefully with Harry, who had become a very vital part of her world. No denying that. Though she was not going to spin rosy dreams about him, as she had with Michael. She would do the realistic thing and live in the moment with Harry.

The moment could not come fast enough today.

She accompanied David back to the office after lunch and they settled in front of the computer workstation to go through the booking system. It took an act of will for Elizabeth to concentrate on it. Anticipation was like a fever in her blood. She kept glancing at the wall clock, wondering how long Harry would stay with Jack and Sarah, aching for him to leave them and come for her.

It had just turned two o'clock when he entered the office, filling it with an electric energy that zapped through every nerve in Elizabeth's body.

'How's it going?' he asked.

'Fine!' Elizabeth managed to clip out.

'Fine!' echoed David.

'Well, I need to have a meeting with Elizabeth now,' Harry said, exuding the alpha male authority that had so surprised her when he'd sacked Sean Cassidy. 'After we leave, you can close the office, David. It doesn't need to be reopened until five o'clock. Take the time to settle in or stroll around, familiarising yourself with the island's attractions. We'll have dinner together this evening.' His arm beckoned commandingly. 'Elizabeth...'

'See you later, David,' she threw at him as she rose from her chair, her heart pounding with excitement at the prospect of spending at least three hours with Harry.

That gave her a lot of moments to live in... to the full.

CHAPTER SEVENTEEN

As soon as they left the office, Harry caught her hand, his long fingers intertwining with hers, gripping possessively, shooting an instant wave of tingling heat up her arm. 'Which villa is yours?' he asked.

'Number one. It's the closest to the office in case I'm needed.'

He smiled at her, his eyes twinkling admiration and approval. 'Standing by,' he said warmly.

'I don't think I'll have to stand by for long, Harry. David's very quick on the uptake.'

He nodded. 'A case of been there, done that. Do you like him?'

'Yes. I think he'll manage very well. He's at ease with the guests, too, eager to please.'

'Good!'

'I doubt he'll need me for more than a few days. When I'm satisfied he's on top of everything I'll come back to Cairns and help you in the office.' She threw him an anxious look, suddenly thinking she might have assumed too much. 'If you want me to.'

He grinned happily. 'I was going to ask if you would. Just to tide us over until Mickey can take control again. Andrew—the guy you suggested could fill in for you—is floundering like a fish out of water under the pressure of too much responsibility. Not his bag at all. Mickey had already directed an agency to find a better replacement for you, but had yet to set up interviews.'

'I'll stay until that can be sorted out,' she promised.

'You wouldn't walk out on anyone at a bad time, would you, Ellie?'

His eyes caressed her as though she was someone very special and her heart fluttered with happiness. 'Not if I could help,' she answered, knowing intuitively that Harry wouldn't, either. He was a caring man who had looked after the people who could have been hurt by Franklyn Finn's sudden death. He hadn't walked away. Not like her father, she thought.

She didn't mind him calling her Ellie anymore. Every time he used that name she heard affection in it, and Harry's affection had become very addictive.

They mounted the steps to the villa's deck. He paused by the railing, his gaze sweeping around the bay below. 'I don't know how Mickey can stand being closed up in an office day after day.'

'He likes running the franchises,' Elizabeth pointed out. 'And since you say he has tunnel vision, I guess that's all he sees when he's there.'

'Mmm…lucky for me! I don't think I could have handled it. I'll be glad when he's back in the driving seat.' His gaze swung to target hers, the blue eyes gathering the intensity that always made her feel he was digging into her mind. 'What about you, Ellie? Have you thought of what you want to do when everything's on course again?'

She shook her head. 'I'm just taking one day at a time.'

'May I make a suggestion?'

'I'm not going to work full-time for you, Harry,' she said quickly, hoping he wouldn't try to persuade her to take up that option again. She had fallen in love with him, and while working together might be great for a while, if he lost his desire for her…

'I wasn't about to ask you to,' he said, drawing her into his embrace.

'What then?' she asked, relieved by this assurance and sliding her hands up his chest, over his shoulders and around his neck, inviting a kiss, wanting him to make love to her, craving intimate contact.

His mouth quirked teasingly. He lifted a hand and gently stroked her cheek, looking deeply into her eyes. 'I don't want you working for me, Ellie. I want you living with me. I'm suggesting that you think about marrying me. We could start a family, make a home together and hopefully live happily ever after. How does that sound?'

She was totally stunned. No way had she anticipated a marriage proposal! Her heart slammed around her chest. She stared at Harry, utterly speechless, barely able to believe what he'd just said.

The shock dilating her eyes told Harry he'd jumped the gun again. This time he didn't care. He wanted her thinking about it, wanted her knowing that he was serious about sharing his future with her. She was *the one* he'd been looking for, *the one* who would complement his life in all the ways that mattered to him. He couldn't bear her having any doubts about where she stood with him.

He had no doubts. This past week had clinched it for him. His brother was no longer a gut-tearing factor in their relationship. That had become clear in all the conversations they'd had. Caring for Mickey had not been at the heart of them. Her focus had been on him—his thoughts, his concerns, his feelings.

He wanted to banish her sense of being adrift, wanted to become *her* anchor, just as she had become his. She might not yet be ready to commit herself to marriage but he saw no harm in laying it on the line. Her mind was clearly rocked at the moment but he didn't sense any negative vibrations coming from her.

'Think about it, Ellie,' he softly commanded, then kissed her.

Elizabeth didn't want to think. She wanted to feel all that Harry made her feel. She threw herself into the kiss, hungry for the wild rush of passion between them—the passion that swept away everything else but the fierce need for each other. It surged through her bloodstream. Her body ached for him, yearned for him, silently but intensely communicating more than she could say.

Harry didn't push for any verbal answer from her. He swept her into the villa and they tore off their clothes, reaching for each other, desire at fever pitch, falling onto the bed, moving urgently to come together. She grasped him with her hands, her legs. He kissed her as the strong shaft of his flesh slid into the pulsating passage that exultantly welcomed their joining. The sheer bliss of it spread through her entire body.

Her mind sang his name...Harry, Harry, Harry....

They rode the waves of pleasure together, driving up the intensity of feeling, instinctively intent on making it more sensational than it had ever been because it was more than physical this time. Much more. Her heart was beating with love for this man, bursting with it as they both climaxed, tipping them over into a world that was uniquely theirs, an intimate sharing that Elizabeth now knew with absolute certainty she would never find with any other man.

It was only a few weeks since she had dreamed of having this with Michael. It seemed weird that in such a short time Harry had so completely supplanted his brother in every sense, but he had. And this was *real*, not a fantasy. She hugged him to her, wanting this *reality* to go on forever.

She thought of Lucy.

Did her sister feel as deeply as this with Michael?

She heaved a sigh, knowing that whatever happened in that relationship was beyond her control.

Harry planted a warm kiss on her forehead. 'Is that a sigh of satisfaction?' he murmured.

'I do love you, Harry,' she said, opening up to him. 'It may seem like an incredible turnaround, but it's true.'

He eased away enough to prop himself up on his elbow and look into her eyes. A smile slowly curved his mouth. 'I love you, too. We're right for each other, Ellie. I know you'll stand by me in all the years to come and I hope you know I'll stand by you.'

'Yes…yes, I do,' she said with certainty.

'So…will you marry me?'

She wanted to.

Lucy would want her to, regardless of what happened with her and Michael. She'd told her so, saying quite vehemently that she didn't want to be the reason for Elizabeth not to have a future with Harry.

Her long hesitation prompted him to ask, 'What reservation do you have in your mind?'

'Will you be kind to Lucy if she and Michael break up?'

It was important to her. She couldn't brush that possibility aside as though it wouldn't count in the future.

He frowned, obviously puzzled that she should be concerned about this. 'Of course I will, Ellie. She's your sister.'

'And Michael's your brother,' she reminded him. 'We could have divided loyalties, Harry.'

'We'll work it out,' he said without hesitation. 'I know Mickey would never interfere with what makes me happy and I bet Lucy would hate feeling she was any kind of block to your having a happy life with me. Am I right about that?'

'Yes,' she conceded, remembering how accurately Harry could read people.

'Then we don't have a problem,' he argued. 'They might not end up together but that won't break our family ties, Ellie. They will both wish us well.'

Yes, she could believe that. It shouldn't be too much of a problem.

'Ellie, we only have one life to live,' Harry pressed on, the intensity back in his eyes. 'We've found each other. Let's not waste time we could have together. You never know when it will be taken away from us.'

Like it had been with his parents.

Like what had almost happened to Michael.

'You're right,' she said, all doubts blown away. 'We should get married. Start having a family. I'm thirty, you know.'

His face broke into a wide grin. 'Yes, I know. And it was the best birthday of all because it brought you to me.'

She laughed, her eyes happily teasing. 'Not very willingly.'

'It was only a matter of time,' he said with arrogant smugness.

She heaved a contented sigh before challenging him one last time, her eyes dancing flirtatiously. 'Well, you're not going to waste any of it, are you? I have to be back at the office…'

His mouth silenced hers.

Her body revelled in having this man.

Her mind was at peace.

She loved Harry Finn and he loved her.

Whatever future they had together they would make the most of it, always being there for each other. That was how it should be and it was going to happen. She and Harry would make it happen because they both wanted it. Everything felt right.

It *was* right.

* * * * *

POSTSCRIPT

Dear Reader,

You have just read Harry's and Elizabeth's story. Michael and Lucy are two entirely different people. While part of their story intersects with this one—their first meeting, the romantic weekend on Finn Island, Michael's car accident—these situations will be related from their points of view in my next book, along with the highs and lows experienced by both of them in their journey towards finding out if they are right for each other. Lust is not love, and passion can turn cold when expectations are not met, when deeply set needs are not answered. The added complications of brothers and sisters can throw shadows, as well, as you've seen in this book. I hope you'll look forward to following the lives of these people. I hope you'll feel for them and want them to end up happily together.

With love always,
Emma Darcy